TUG OF WAR

Icy waters that froze a torpedoed sailor within minutes ... frozen metal that would tear the flesh from a man's hands ... screaming blizzards that whipped the sea to a white fury. This was the dreaded convoy run from Hull to Murmansk, through Arctic seas patrolled by Hitler's U-boats. Into this hell went HMS *Rattlesnake,* a First World War tugboat that had already been sold once for the scrapheap. What her crew did not know was that their route had already been betrayed to the Germans, and the U-boats were waiting...

TUG OF WAR

TUG OF WAR

by

Duncan Harding

Dales Large Print Books
Long Preston, North Yorkshire,
BD23 4ND, England.

British Library Cataloguing in Publication Data.

Harding, Duncan
Tug of war.

A catalogue record of this book is available from the British Library

ISBN 1-84262-298-6 pbk

First published in Great Britain in 1976 by Seeley Service & Co.

Cover illustration by arrangement with G.B. Print Ltd.

Published in Large Print 2004 by arrangement with Eskdale Publishing

Dales Large Print is an imprint of Library Magna Books Ltd.

Printed and bound in Great Britain by
T.J. (International) Ltd., Cornwall, PL28 8RW

'NORTHWARD AND NETHERWARD LIES THE PATH TO HELL'

–Old Norse Proverb

INTRODUCTION

'The worst voyage in the world,' Winston Churchill called it in 1942. He meant the convoy run between Hull and the Russian port of Murmansk which enabled the British and other Allied navies to supply vital war goods to war-torn Soviet Union between 1941 and 1944.

The men who sailed those ships in the Merchant and the Royal Navies had other, more earthy descriptions for those convoys. One which could be printed was 'a hell below zero'. For the battles those seamen fought so long ago were not only against the German enemy; they were also against the elements. Arctic winds which could whip a lookout's face into the colour of an underdone steak; icy waters that froze the torpedoed sailor to death within minutes; frozen metal that ripped the flesh off men's hands in bloody chunks if they were foolish enough to touch it without gloves.

Off Bear Island alone, more than ten thousand British and Allied seamen died trying to sail through the 'gate' into the Barents Sea; more Allied sailors than anywhere else in the world. It was the graveyard of the Arctic.

In 1942 it was said that if you sailed through the 'gate' and came back again, you were a lucky man. If you did that terrible voyage more than a couple of times, you'd had all the luck you were ever going to have in a whole long lifetime.

This is the story of thirty men from England's East Coast, who not only fought the 'hell below zero', but also tried to sail through that dreaded gate. It is also the story of those Germans from another barren coast, who lurked beneath the icy grey waters and tried to stop them. It is, in short, the tale of a terrible ten-day long tug-of-war, in which there were no victors, only victims.

DAY ONE: DECEMBER 22nd, 1941

'The Humber is the arsehole of the world and Hull is some place stuffed right up it!'

Anonymous Hull Businessman

Hartmann hit the flat muddy stretch of Yorkshire coast at 400 mph. Across the bay at the Point, the Tommy flak opened up. But it was too late. By the time the Tommies had located him, his 109E was streaking down Withernsea's shabby main street, scattering the women queuing up in front of the little shops.

Oberstleutnant Hartmann's Messerschmitt roared on. Across the white-frozen winter fields ahead he could see the tall steel aerials of Patrington's RAF radar station. Down below, in the station's underground system, pale-faced women in uniform – 'field mattresses' as the Luftwaffe pilots called them contemptuously – would now be hurriedly placing his fighter on the plot. But again they would be too late. By the time they had scrambled the fighters around

York, his lone tip-and-run raider would be long gone. Ever since he had his leg shot off by a Spitfire pilot over Dover in the summer of 1941, he had taken great care in planning this sort of mission.

Patrington disappeared behind him. A farmer digging in a steaming manure heap below, straightened up and waved to him. But when he saw the great black crosses on the plane's wings, his wave changed to an angry shake of his clenched fist. Hartmann dropped twenty metres suddenly. The farmer panicked and plunged headfirst into the dark-yellow mess. Hartmann chuckled, but the cold light in his blue eyes did not vanish. He flew on at tree-top height, while a machine-gun chattered angrily below. The Luftwaffe pilot did not even notice it.

To his right he spotted what he was looking for – the grey Gothic bulk of Hedon church which seemed far too large for the huddle of little red-brick houses surrounding it. He couldn't hope for a better landmark. It was like a signpost pointing the way to Hull.

Oberstleutnant Hartmann threw a quick glance around his instrument panel. *Alles in Ordung.* He settled himself more comfortably in his seat and checked his rear mirror. It was blank. No nasty Tommy on his tail.

'Well, here we go then – into the next waltz,' he said to himself.

He flashed at 400 mph down the dead straight road that led from Hedon to his target – Hull docks. On his left there was the flat, dull green water of the estuary; to his right the bomb-shattered houses of the dock workers. A long line of canvas-covered trucks came into view.

'More supplies for Ivan!' he cursed through clenched teeth.

Automatically, his gloved thumb pressed the fire button. The fighter shuddered as eight machine-guns burst into life. Red and white tracer sped towards the slow-moving trucks. At that range he could not miss. He could even see the bullets ripping their canvas covers. The convoy came to a sudden stop and just as he roared over the leader, one of the trucks exploded. He could not hear the sound, but the blast threw his plane up a good fifty metres.

'High octane fuel,' Hartmann told himself joyfully.

Behind him, as the drivers scattered for cover, the convoy began to burn fiercely. But the one-legged fighter ace had already forgotten it. His cold eyes were now fixed on the confused mess of masts and funnels ahead, his quick brain working out which would be the best targets for his two five hundred pound bombs.

He came in low with the sun behind him. A machine-gun opened up somewhere in the docks. He could see the white tracer accelerating through the air towards him. Bullets struck his wing like heavy summer rain on a tin roof. Still he concentrated on his target: a long Norwegian tanker, with men scattering wildly across its massive deck as he hurtled in for the attack. He pressed the bomb toggle. The plane lurched and rose a sudden one hundred metres. He brought it under control and tore into the sky.

Below him, the tanker erupted. One moment it was a solid line of metal; the next, two great halves rearing upwards, scattering men into the water like insects. Hartmann chuckled at his own reflection in the rear mirror. He had got the bastard.

As the tanker began to burn fiercely, sending up a huge pillar of thick oily black smoke into the grey winter sky, Hartmann set off for home. But since that terrible July day when he had seen his own booted foot lying in the sticky red mess on the floor of his cockpit, he had become careful. He knew that now the whole of Humberside would be alerted to the lone raider. He knew too that at the Point and on the other side of the Humber at Immingham, the Tommy flak concentrations would already be ranged in, waiting for him to appear. Most inexperienced pilots used the Humber as a navigational aid on their way back to their bases in Holland. But Oberstleutnant Hartmann was a veteran – Spain with the Condor Legion in '37, Poland in '39, France and Britain in '40 – he would not fly into the Tommy guns.

Thus it was that Hartmann made the great discovery. Roaring in low over the King George V Dock with the flat sluggish expanse of the Humber ahead of him, he was just about to break right to fool the Tommies by flying inland, when he saw them. From the lock-gate right up to the mouth of the estuary one merchantman after another was being shepherded into place by a lean cocky frigate.

'*Ach du grosse Kacke am Christbaum!*' Hartmann swore.

He broke right and flew over the dirty water, his monstrous black shadow hurrying ahead of him. As soon as he reached the old-fashioned railway bridge across the

Humber, he would swing into Lincolnshire and cross the coast there, out of the range of the Humber defences and before the Tommy fighters from York could react. But now he had to report his amazing stroke of luck.

Just as Home Guardsman Charlie Broke, ex-Fourth Battalion, King's Own Yorkshire Light Infantry, took the low-flying Messerschmitt into the sights of his World War One Lewis gun, Hartmann broke his radio silence.

'Bertha, Arthur, Martha here – hallo, Control … come in Control!' he called urgently.

Control Alpen answered almost immediately.

'Hallo Bertha, Arthur, Martha … Control here. Hearing you loud and clear. Over!'

Scarcely able to contain his excitement, Hartmann passed on his news.

'And tell the boys of the Fifth Air Fleet in Norway from me,' he added joyfully, 'That my wing gets a case of champagne for every Tommy that they sink!'

Down below, Guardsman Broke could not believe his own eyes as the Jerry fighter grew larger and larger within the big ring sight of the machine-gun.

'Bloody hell, Joe,' he breathed to his

number two, Big Daft Joe Mercer, who worked with him in the sugarbeet factory at Selby, 'yon silly bugger's gonna commit suicide!'

Nevertheless he did not forget the old days at Amiens in 1918. He tucked the wooden butt firmly into his shoulder, took a deep breath and began to squeeze the trigger nice and gently, 'as if you was having a right good feel at yer lady friend,' the sergeant-instructor (musketry) had bellowed in '16. 'Not scratching yer hairy arses!'

'And tell the Fifth, we don't want any of your crappy Moselle Sekt, but real French champus,' Hartmann was saying when Broke pressed the trigger.

The Messerschmitt was a sitting target. Hartmann felt a bullet fracture the radiator's coolant system. A rending explosion. The fighter was enveloped in a white, choking cloud of blinding glycol steam. Hastily Hartmann undid his safety straps. Fighting the screaming pressure as the Messerschmitt went into a dive, the German ace raised himself in the cockpit, peering over the top of the shattered windscreen. The muddy flats of the Humber were racing up to meet him at a tremendous speed. Charlie Broke's finger curled over the trigger again, as he followed the stricken German down.

'Get ready to change the pan, Joe,' he ordered.

'For crying out loud – give him a chance, Charlie!' Big Daft Joe shouted. 'Tha's given him a bellyful... Yon poor sod's had it anyroad.'

'The only good Hun's a dead Hun,' Broke replied, remembering a phrase he had not used these twenty years and pressed the trigger again.

The machine-gun kicked at his shoulder once more. As the fresh stream of bullets ripped along the length of the plane, Hartmann fell back into the burning cockpit. On the instrument panel, the red lights flickered on and off alarmingly. Dying slowly, pressed against the headrest by the force of gravity, Hartmann watched them detachedly as the Messerschmitt raced towards the mud flats at 500 mph. How easy it was to die, he thought. All that fuss, that training, the heartache, the years of preparation just for this – a swift end on some obscure piece of Tommyland miles from his native Hamburg. Oberstleutnant Hartmann, Knight's Cross with Diamonds, closed his eyes and resigned himself to the end in the knowledge that the Tommies would pay a hundredfold for his death.

Trailing a huge banner of red flame behind it, the Messerschmitt hit one of the Humber's muddy banks. Its fuel tanks burst into flame with a tremendous roar. Tracer ammunition zig-zagged crazily upwards. As the little tumbledown holding began to burn to the accompaniment of the pigs' squeals, the blind woman called eerily:

'Have we got him … have we got him?'

The explosion slopped the luke-warm, grey water out of the enamel bowl in front of the flickering coal fire on to the day-old copy of the *Hull Daily Mail* on which it rested.

'You can't even get a sodding bath in peace without them sodding Jerries having a go at you', snapped Chief Petty Officer Thirsk, and raised his flannel as if he would like to use it on the German who had interrupted his washdown.

'You could use the bath, George,' his wife Meg said, knitting on the chair opposite. 'You don't have to wash in front of the kitchen hearth.'

'Are you crackers?' CPO Thirsk said. 'You know that it's highly dangerous to get cold water on yer back! You can catch yer death like that. I thought you had enough common to know that?' His leathery face cracked into a slow smile. 'Besides it has an effect on yer sex life – cold water. It's as bad as them down-boy pills they gave us in the First War when I was a recruit. You wouldn't like yer husband to end up as a singing tenor, would you?'

Meg Thirsk looked up at her husband's skinny body.

'Listen at him! You get yer share, don't you?'

'I should hope so,' the CPO said, stepping out of the bowl. 'Give us the towel. I don't want to leave it all to your fancy man. Before they punch me cards, I'd like to get a little bit of the other. There's not much a poor sailorman gets out of this life anyhow.'

'You get your share, George Thirsk,' his wife said, flushing faintly and passed him the towel, which had been warming on the hearth. 'There you are – and cover that nasty thing up, will you? What if your son came down and saw you standing like that? What would he think?'

'You don't think he only uses it to pee with, do you, Meg? What do you think he's down at the Mecca for every night that he's on leave – to have a bit of a chat about Stephen Spender or something?'

'Who's he when he's at home?'

'Don't worry your poor simple woman's head about him,' her husband said, 'pass me them bandages instead.'

Meg Thirsk handed her husband the thick crepe bandages which had been warming next to the towel in front of the hearth, hanging from the chocolate box which their son Peter had brought home in 1935 when the Hull Education Committee had given every pupil a box as a memento of George V's Jubilee. Swiftly he began to bind them round his crippled knees.

While he was doing so, Meg Thirsk began to pick at the corner of the plaster, trying to get her thumb nail under it.

'Is it proper Wintergreen?' Her husband asked, finished with his knees. 'There's nothing like a real Wintergreen to keep your kidneys warm off the North Cape.'

'The chemist said this one would burn the ballocks off'n a bull,' she said, succeeding finally in getting her nail between the plaster and its cover.

CPO Thirsk's mouth dropped open.

'Mr Smithers said that?'

'No, you daft bugger. He wouldn't say anything like that. You're the only one who'd use that kind of language around here.'

'Oh, aye. All right, slap the bugger on.'

Meg Thirsk smoothed the plaster on to her husband's skinny back. He shivered and shrugged his shoulders several times.

'Sodding cold,' he said. 'But it'll get warm in a couple of minutes. All right, where's me shirt?'

Meg Thirsk shook her head.

'What would you do without me, George Thirsk?' she asked.

He advanced upon her, as naked as he was, moving stiff-legged because of the bandages which were the only things which kept his rheumatic pains at bay when he was at sea. With surprising tenderness he enfolded her in his skinny arms and said; 'I don't know, Meg. Now what do you say to us having a little drink before the Thirsk family goes back to sea?'

His leathery face looked so old that tears shot to Meg's eyes. Suddenly she remembered him the way he had looked as he had first pushed open the door of the 'Mucky Duck' – the Black Swan pub in George Street – in 1919, his big chest full of ribbons, his cap at the back of his head, his white teeth gleaming like an advertisement for Gibbs toothpaste, full of 'wind and piss', as he had described himself in the years that had followed. Now his chest had become sunken, the gleaming black hair grey and the white teeth had been bought from the Panel at one-and-six per week. Protectively she pressed his skinny rheumaticky body to her ample breast.

'Now then, George Thirsk,' she forced herself to say. 'Whoever heard of anybody in Hull having an ale before dinnertime? You've got a long trip in front of you. You don't want to start getting yer pipes overheated before you get underway.'

The old secret phrase had its effect. Slowly he released her full body from his arms, thinking, as he had done often during this last leave, how old she had become.

'Ay, yer right, old lass, it's a long way to Murmansk. It wouldn't do to get yer knickers twisted before you got out of the King George Fifth dock, would it now?'

Slowly CPO Thirsk began to hide his worn body in the uniform he had worn so proudly these last thirty years. By the time that Peter Thirsk, fourth officer in the pride of the Ellerman Wilson Line, the SS *St George*, the fastest ship in Convoy PQ 8, came downstairs to tell his parents that he would rejoin the tanker in Scotland, CPO Thirsk looked as a senior petty officer of the

Royal Navy should look: lean, trim, efficient and completely without fear.

The London train had just begun to clatter across the old iron railway bridge over the Humber outside Goole when a sudden explosion rocked the carriage alarmingly. Lieutenant Andrews, coming to the end of *They Died with their Boots on* started, then flushed when he saw that the fat, pasty-faced businessman was watching him over the top of the *Yorkshire Post.*

'What was that damned noise?' he asked immediately and made a show of adjusting his black tie to cover up his embarrassment.

'Hull,' the businessman said. 'Hull's probably getting a packet again, I expect.'

'I see,' Andrews said, as usual not knowing quite what to say. 'Jerry, what?'

'Yes, *Jerry,*' the fat businessman was mimicking his accent. 'Ever since the Russkis came into the war, the Germans have been knocking the stuffing out of us. Before then, all that you Southerners knew about the place was that ... that the Humber was the arsehole of the world – and Hull was some place stuffed right up it!'

He said the words without rancour. All the same Andrews flushed again. He didn't like to hear that sort of talk; it embarrassed him. But the fat businessman did not seem to notice.

'Now the Jerries have to put us on the map in Hull – by trying to knock the sodding place off it!'

'Is it that bad?' Andrews asked sympathetically.

'Ay, it is, London is a tea party in comparison.' For the first time, the businessman took in the spick new naval uniform. 'Murmansk run, eh? Your first time?'

Again Lieutenant Andrew Andrews coloured. It was something he was always doing, with superior officers, ratings, girls – especially girls – but he couldn't seem to prevent it happening. He pointed to the grubby warning poster next to the yellowed Victorian photograph of Scarborough on the carriage wall.

'Careless talk costs lives.'

The fat man laughed.

'Don't kid yourself, Lieutenant. Half the street-walkers in Hull and Grimsby know more about the Murmansk sailings than your bosses at the Admiralty. When those merchant navy lads get in the knocking shops off Hedon Road, they like to run off at the lip to show what heroes they are.

Look at me, for instance, Lieutenant. I'm a buyer for a woodyard near the docks. I've no special source of information, but I could give a damn good guess at what you'll be doing in the next few weeks. You'll rendezvous with a convoy somewhere off the west coast of Iceland, where the heavy escorts will join you. Then you'll make your way past Bear Island into the Barents Sea and the heavy boys will leave you.' He chuckled humourlessly. 'Abandon you, some of the merchant skippers would say. Because it's just there that the Jerries will start plastering you. First the bombers from Norway, then the surface raiders – and what they don't get, the subs will.' He paused and sighed. 'You see, even I know.'

Before Andrews could answer, their attention was attracted by a burning Messerschmitt which had apparently crashed into a small holding on the mud bank of the estuary. Already the Home Guard were beginning to throw a cordon round it to keep away the souvenir hunters and the looters.

'Well, that's one Jerry less, sir, at least,' Andrews remarked cheerfully. 'He won't be dropping any more bombs on your Hull.'

'Plenty more where he came from,' said

his companion dourly.

The young naval officer shrugged and turned to stare out of the dirty window at the grubby rows of nineteenth century terrace-housing which heralded Kingston-upon-Hull, while the fat businessman surveyed him out of the corner of his eye. A very young man in a very proud uniform, who looked as if he were not quite sure if he were entitled to it. It was just the way his own son John had looked the day he'd sailed from Hull on his first Murmansk run. He'd never come back.

Minutes later the London train was steaming into Hull. Paragon Street station was full of the hustle and bustle of wartime; keen-eyed Redcaps waiting at the barriers on the lookout for deserters; self-important RTO officers striding officiously down the platform; the local prostitutes idling in the shadows, waiting for customers; and everywhere streams of pale-faced sailors, kitbags slung over their shoulders, artificial silk scarves knotted around their open necks, heading for the blue-painted buses which would take them down the docks, caught up once again in the terrible machinery of the Murmansk run.

'All right, lads, let's have you out! Lively now!' Petty Officer Erickson struck the canvas side of the truck with his calloused hand.

'Come on now, get yer fingers out. We're going to march the rest of the way.'

There were some groans and grumbles from within the three-tonner.

'I'll catch my death walking in this weather, Chief,' someone called.

'The recruiting officer told me that you never walked in the Navy.'

'Complain to the chaplain, sailor,' Erickson growled, but his tough face, burnt a permanent brick-red by the Arctic winds, cracked into a smile. Sailors were always the same: they never liked to walk.

As the pale leavemen dropped to the dockside and saw the snarl of hose-pipes which were pumping water to the burning Norwegian tanker, they could see that the truck wouldn't be able to go any further.

'Sodding hell,' a leading rating cursed as he saw the pillar of black oily smoke which reached up three hundred feet or more in the grey December sky. 'Jerry gave him some stick, didn't he!'

'Ay, that's why the tanker crews get nice soft beds and cinema shows aboard, me lad,'

Erickson snapped. ''Cos they're sitting on a load of dynamite all the time they're at sea. All right, get fell in now. We'll try this navy style.'

Again there was some grumbling, but those crew of HMS *Rattlesnake,* who knew that PO Erickson (a £2,000 a year cod skipper with his own ship off Iceland before the war) had refused the rank of Skipper-Lieutenant, RNR to stay in the lower deck, also knew that he was no friend of traditional Royal Navy bull. Erickson was a man who wanted to get a job done efficiently and smartly. If the new captain did happen to be on board the *Rattlesnake* and they straggled up to it looking like a lot of Hull civvies there'd probably be hell to pay.

'All right, pick up yer gear,' the Petty Officer snapped when they'd formed up in a rough and ready line. 'Right turn by left, quick march!'

Staggering under their loads and stumbling over the debris from the air raid and the hose-pipes they started to march towards the *Rattlesnake,* while the ancient dockyard fire-engines and the newer ones of the Auxiliary Fire Service rattled back and forth, trying to extinguish the flames in the stricken Norwegian tanker.

CPO Thirsk was waiting for them at the foot of the gangway. Despite the icy wind from the North Sea which was blowing along the dust-dry quayside, he was without a greatcoat. He stood there watching them, trim and erect, as if he were standing on the quarter of the old *Warspite,* his faded blue eyes humorous but wary. One of the dockers sheltering with his mates between the crates, hands cupped round an illegal Woodbine farted loudly and called:

'Watch it, lads, here comes the Royal Navy!'

CPO Thirsk looked across at him, as if he were one of the grey dockside rats which were always poking their heads among the great port's debris, and then bellowed:

'All right, you pregnant ducks, let's see you swing them arms! Open them legs. Bags of swank now! Remember you're the elite, the new rich, with one bob a day hard lying allowance! Not like yer docker struggling on with a tenner a week and what he can nick from government stores!'

Erickson halted the party and reported to CPO Thirsk, as if he were back on the square at HMS *Lochinvar.* Thirsk acknowledged it with a brisk nod of his grey head.

'Thank you, Erickson... All right, party –

party, stand at ease! Stand easy!'

There was a shuffle of feet and a few groans of relief as the ratings dropped their kitbags on to the dockside. For a moment Thirsk did nothing but gaze along their young faces, checking those who had sailed with him on the *Rattlesnake*'s last trip. There weren't so many of them. Ten days of towing a burning grain ship from Bear Island to Murmansk had been enough for most of them. They'd either gone sick or wangled a posting to the mine-sweeping service. The men facing him were those of the old crew who were too stupid to work their ticket, or new recruits who had just finished their advance training on HMS *Lochinvar*.

'All right,' he barked, 'listen to me! Bunts and Sparks, you've heard all this before. You can fall out and stow away your gear.'

The leading telegraphist and the signals rating who had been with him on *Rattlesnake*'s last trip fell out and hurried up the gangway, glad to get out of the biting wind.

'The rest of you get this. My name is Thirsk and I've been in the Royal over twenty-five years.' He poked a thick thumb at his immaculate tunic, now already stuffed with medicated cotton-wool to keep the cold out. 'When you lot was still filling yer nappies, I was in the China Station, eating filleted Chink for breakfast.'

He looked along their trembling pale-faced ranks grimly.

'I've been everywhere,' he continued, 'done everything and seen everything. So there's no use coming the madam with me. Any kind of lead-swinging with me and I'll have you in the nick so quick yer short-arsed legs won't even touch the sodding deck. Isn't that right, Petty Officer?'

'That's right Chief!' Erickson barked loyally and tried not to smile as he remembered the seventeen year old ordinary seaman whom Thirsk had nursed right throughout the last trip, even doing the boy's kitchen chores when the kid had been sick at the very sight of the breakfast 'soya links.'

'All right, as long as you lot of mother's darlings play ball with me, I'll play ball with you.' CPO Thirsk's voice lost its gruffness. 'I know it's cold lads,' he went on. 'So I won't be much longer. I'm supposed to read the Articles of War to you lot before you come aboard. There's a damn lot of 'em and I've no doubt that most of you Oxford men wouldn't understand 'em if I did. So I'll say this. They mean you're now at war and that tub behind me,' he pointed his thumb over his shoulder at the rusting deep-sea tug, with the white ensign flying at her bow, 'is yer home from now onwards. When we go to sea, we're in for a lot of hard work and perhaps a bit of danger. I was blowed up twice in the first lot and I've had a packet in this one. So you can expect trouble. But if you do yer duty and work the best you can, me and the Captain'll see that you get yer full privileges when we get back to port.'

'If we get back,' Erickson thought.

'So that's all the Articles of War is about. 'All right, look to your front. Party–'

'Chief Petty Officer,' Erickson cut in hastily.

'Yes?'

'Well, sir, could you tell them about the rabbits and–' Erickson was suddenly embarrassed.

CPO Thirsk chuckled.

'All right, Erickson, don't wet yer skivvies – I'll tell them.' He turned to the crew again. 'One last thing. Some of you lads'll be from the town and like and so what I'm going to say might seem a bit funny to you. But I want you all to take it deadly serious. The kind of hand you usually find on ships like the *Rattlesnake* are from the East Coast, fishing men like Petty Officer Erickson here or like Bunts and Sparks who've just gone aboard. And fishermen are superstitious – I'd be too if I had to earn my living by fishing. It's just a fact of life for them. So,' he glared at the crew, who were now shivering violently in the wind, 'I don't want the words "pig", "fox", or "rabbit" mentioned again once you're aboard ship. Nor do I want to see anybody putting a hatch-cover on upside down or anyone laying a broom across a hawser, do you hear?'

'Why, Chief?' a big sailor in the front rank asked.

Thirsk crossed over to him and thrust his tough old leathery face close to the rating's.

'City lad, eh? Well, I'll tell you why, sailor. Because if you do, it'll bring bad luck.' He lowered his voice significantly. 'And more than likely the whole ship'll disappear without a trace. That's what happened to the *Sprite* in forty after the Second Hand smuggled a couple of rabbits aboard for Christmas Dinner. They never found hair nor hide of the *Sprite*'s crew.'

'Go on, Chief,' the big man said doubtfully, 'you're pulling me pisser!'

As the crew started to file up the gangplank, Thirsk winked at Petty Officer

Erickson conspiratorially. But the ex-fishing boat skipper did not return the wink. However Thirsk might mock, he knew that it was not just superstition; let anyone just mention those words on board and HMS *Rattlesnake* was as good as sunk.

The Flag-Officer-in-Charge, Hull, Vice-Admiral Fox-Talbot, was a big man, broad and tough-looking. He was about forty-eight, his hair greying, with deep lines at the corner of his grey eyes, the products of good-humour, cynicism and three decades of sea-going, he looked to Lieutenant Andrews like the ideal Royal Navy officer: an ideal he would never achieve even if he lived to be a hundred.

'Andrews,' he said, looking up from the pile of papers on his big desk. 'Two years RNVR.' He sniffed. 'Mucking about with boats, I suppose?'

'Ay ay, sir. The Solent. I joined up as a rating in '40 and was sent to *King Alfred.*'

'I see. Well, Andrews, you've got your first command at a ripe old age, haven't you? Exactly twenty-two. I was eight years older than you before I got mine.'

'It's only a tug, sir.'

'A tug.' The Vice-Admiral frowned. 'A

crew of twenty-nine human beings, you mean, Andrews, with all their various appendages – wives, sweethearts, mothers, nippers, etc. And all in your hands at the ripe old age of twenty-two. It's a lot of responsibility, believe me.'

Outside a fire-engine clattered by, bell ringing, and drowned even the maddening chatter of the typewriters in the ops room outside.

'I know, sir,' Andrews ventured when it had passed. 'I'm sorry, sir.'

'Never be sorry, Andrews – at least publicly. Do what you think is right and keep your fingers crossed that you are. But never apologize.'

'No, sir.'

Suddenly Vice-Admiral Fox-Talbot's face cracked into a brilliant smile.

'Come on now, don't look so worried about it. It was only a piece of advice and not an Admiralty order. Now let me tell you briefly your job, Andrews. This morning Convoy PQ 8 sailed from the Humber on the Murmansk run. It'll sail the usual route – Iceland, Bear Island, the Barents Sea, etc. According to our wallahs in Naval Intelligence it should have an easy run most of the way. Jerry's surface raiders are all in the Baltic and the two pocket battleships they've got on the French coast don't appear to be getting ready to sail.'

He paused. Outside in the ops room someone was saying in a high-pitched, hysterical voice:

'So I told him, you can't expect to get promotion again after only a year in grade... But it's the kind of thing you expect from these wavy navy chaps, don't you!'

'The trouble will start once you're past Bear Island, Andrews,' the Admiral continued. His smile had vanished now and for the first time the young officer could see just how tired he was. 'That's where the balloon will go up – it always does. Now it'll be your task to follow the convoy into the Barents Sea and pick up any casualty you think is seaworthy enough to get to Murmansk. In particular, keep your eyes open for tankers and munition ships. You see, Andrews,' he leaned back in his leather chair a little, 'whatever you think about the Bolshies – and I don't think much, because I fought against them in 1918 – they are taking the main brunt of the land fighting and we've got to help them keep in the war. Everything – anything – that gets through to them is of vital importance, even woolly bedsocks for their wounded. Do you understand?'

'Ay, ay, sir.'

'Good,' Vice-Admiral Fox-Talbot picked up his simple wooden pen again. 'Not that you'll get much help from them. The Red Fleet is usually conspicuous by its absence and you'll not see a single Bolshy plane till you're practically in Kola Bay.' He looked down at his lists again. 'All right, Andrews, you'd better be getting to your ship now. And the best of luck!'

'Thank you, sir!' Lieutenant Andrews snapped to attention and gave his best *King Alfred* salute.

The Admiral did not look up, but as the young officer went out, he put a quick tick against Andrews' name on the list and made a mental note of his face so that he wouldn't forget who the young officer was when he came to write the letter of condolence to his next-of-kin.

With the ancient CPO who was going to act as his second-in-command at his side, Lieutenant Andrews picked his way across the dock towards his ship. There was noise and bustle everywhere: the crash of steel hawsers, the discordant rattle of cranes and derricks, the insane nerve-wracking chatter of the riveters' guns, as the dockers and the dockyard workers prepared yet another convoy for the Murmansk run. Conversation was almost impossible so they remained silent until Andrews caught the first real sight of his new command as they rounded the corner of a warehouse. He gasped. Cupping his hands round his mouth, he yelled:

'Is that the *Rattlesnake,* Chief?'

Thirsk nodded.

Andrews stared at the ocean-going tug in dismay. Specked with rust, its tall funnel covered with peeling camouflaged paint, HMS *Rattlesnake* looked as if she might have been a battered hulk salvaged from the bottom of the sea; only the dripping seaweed and the barnacles were missing.

'Am I responsible for taking *that* to sea, Chief?' he cried.

CPO Thirsk forced a smile; the new skipper did not look a day older than his own son. He'd have to help him.

'Don't worry, sir,' he yelled above the noise as they began to mount the gangway. 'She's a lot tougher than she looks.'

Andrews did not reply for a moment. One good Arctic wind, he told himself feeling frightened, and HMS *Rattlesnake* looked as if she would go straight to the bottom. Then he became aware of the furtive glances the deck ratings were giving him, and he pulled himself together.

'Better show me my cabin, Chief,' he said, 'and tell me a little about her.'

Five minutes later they were seated in his 'cabin', a steel tank, cold, clammy and smelling of fuel oil, separated from the corridor by a heavy canvas black-out curtain, and CPO Thirsk was rattling off HMS *Rattlesnake*'s vital statistics.

'She's one hundred and fifty-six feet overall, sir, with a gross weight of six hundred and fifty-three tons. Her engine is a 1,200 hp-triple expansion – that's big enough to power a five-thousand ton freighter, sir. Her range is about twenty days under full power, though we did one day over that on the last trip to Murmansk. What else?' CPO Thirsk thought for a moment. 'Heavy duty towing winch – and accommodation for twenty-six, though with you, sir, we've got thirty.'

'Hence my own palatial accommodation, Chief, eh?' Lieutenant Andrews grinned, looking round the miserable little cabin, bare of any decoration save a calendar for 1940 and a faded photograph of an elderly woman with snow-white hair. 'Lieutenant Skinner's sir,' the CPO explained. 'The last skipper. He bought it just as we was getting into Kola Bay. I forgot it when I was clearing up his things.'

'I see.'

CPO Thirsk knew what the young officer must be thinking and he hurried on.

'This class of tug was something very new at the time when the Admiralty commissioned them. A seaboat first and then a tug. But the class came too late for the First War. She never saw any action. All she did was to tow a few old warships into Scapa and then was sold for scrap to the Yanks.'

'Scrap? How did we get her then?'

CPO Thirsk grinned.

'For a bit of Bermuda on a ninety-nine year lease. Remember that business in Forty, sir when the Yankees swapped us fifty destroyers?'

'Yes. Did they throw in the *Rattlesnake* for good measure too, Chief?'

'You might say so, sir. The old *Rattlesnake*'s seen a lot in her time, sir. A boat like this takes nothing from the sea; it sort of sneaks up on what it wants and wiggles it away again. If you was to ask me, sir, I'd say it isn't old Jerry who's the main enemy for a ship like this, it's the sea–'

He broke off suddenly. A hard fist

hammered on the bulkhead outside.

'Come in!' Andrews yelled.

Petty Officer Erickson flung back the blackout curtain, his face flushed an even deeper red, his eyes sparkling with anger.

'Petty Officer Erickson, sir,' CPO Thirsk introduced the other non-commissioned officer.

'Hello, Erickson,' Andrews said hesitantly. He still hadn't got the hang of addressing petty officers correctly; his terror of them during his days on the lower deck had not yet vanished. 'Please take a seat, if you can find one. Now what is it?'

But Erickson, a man who had skippered his own boat since he was eighteen and tamed a bunch of East Coast fishermen twice his age, had no time for social niceties just at that moment. He remained standing, his big fist clenched.

'It's them ruddy thieving dockies, sir!' he exploded. 'I was just checking the Carley floats – just in case.'

CPO Thirsk indicated to his junior to be quiet for a moment while he explained.

'On the last run, sir, we thought we might have to abandon ship. The grain ship it was towing looked as if it was going to go up after the Heinkels had finished with it – and take us with it. So I told Petty Officer Erickson here to make sure that they were in order this time.'

'Yessir! And they weren't! The dockies had left the water all right.' Erickson's almost crimson face twisted scornfully. 'Oh, yes, they'd leave us with the water. But both tins of provisions have gone and you don't need to be no Gypsy Rose Lee to know where them tins have gone – down George Street into the black market! The thieving bastards! While we're risking our necks for them, they're flogging our bit of food which might mean all the difference between coming out alive or not if we have to use them floats!' His jaw hardened, 'Hull dockies – they've always been the same! By Christ, if I had my way, I'd–'

'But you haven't, Erickson,' CPO Thirsk interrupted calmly. 'So don't go rupturing yourself worrying about it. Them Hull civvies have always been like that and they allus will be, long after they've planted you in Brown's garden.' He turned to Andrews and said softly: 'While we're in the lock, sir, I'll double over to the dockyard superintendent. If his office has any spare grub he'll let me have it. I know him well. That is with your permission, sir?'

'Of course, of course,' Andrews said hastily.

CPO Thirsk rose stiffly from his seat; his bloody knees were beginning to ache already and they weren't even into the Humber yet. He gave Erickson a curt nod and the disgruntled petty officer slipped away. The CPO waited till he was out of earshot.

'Sir, just one more thing.'

'Yes?'

CPO Thirsk fumbled with his cap and hesitated as he looked down at the young skipper.

'Well, sir, it's a bit hard to know where to begin.'

'At the beginning, Chief.'

'All right, sir, and I hope you won't be offended. All I want to say is that the old *Rattlesnake* don't look much, especially to a young officer like yourself. She's no fancy frigate or S-class destroyer, that's for certain. But she was built to work hard – and die hard too, if necessary.'

'I'm sure of that, Chief,' Andrews replied a little embarrassed at the old petty officer's obvious emotion. 'It's just that she didn't look much at first sight.'

CPO Thirsk did not seem to hear.

'And begging your leave, sir, if you need any help – well, I'd always be glad to do the best I can.'

Before Andrews could reply, the CPO had clicked to attention, swung round and was gone, leaving the black-out curtain swaying behind him.

Slowly the significance of the older man's words dawned on him. Andrew Andrews realized, for the first time since he had been commissioned, that he had found an ally against the alarming world of gold-ringed officialdom, as well as the still more daunting future that waited in the cold North Sea beyond the mouth of the Humber, and the young skipper began to feel happier.

Two hours later HMS *Rattlesnake* had left the lock and had entered the estuary, nosing her way down the grey littered channel. On the little bridge, Andrews could feel the wind from the sea biting his face. He buried his head deeper into the collar of his duffle-coat and marvelled at a couple of the deck ratings who were still moving about with the sleeves of their dungarees rolled up, as if it were mid-summer, singing over and over again the same monotonous refrain:

'I've got spurs that jingle, jangle, jingle
As I go riding merr-i-lee along.'

Andrews turned to stare at the Yorkshire bank of the estuary. The early winter dusk was beginning to close in, hiding the ugly mud-banks and broad line of shingle which stretched as far as the Point. At that moment, with the illuminated buoys and the shore lights beginning to blink everywhere, the harsh northern vista was almost beautiful. Beautiful or not, he told himself, it would be his last sight of England for a month – or even longer, but that was a possibility one didn't even dare think about.

'Sir.' It was Leading-Signalman Turner, 'Bunts', as the rest of the crew called him, a smart young fisherman from Grimsby, who might well have been a yeoman of signals by now, if, as Andrews knew from a quick glance at his crime sheet that afternoon, he hadn't had a disastrously strong liking for the local ale.

'What is it, Turner?'

His feet just slightly apart to counteract the faint swell, his pad and pencil held ready, the very model of an efficient signalman, he said officiously.

'I thought you'd like to send the signal, sir.'

'Signal?' Then he remembered. 'Of course.

Thank you for reminding me, Turner.'

Turner waited dutifully, pencil poised, but there was a faint smile of self-congratulation on his thin face. Andrews licked his lips and began to dictate his first message from his own ship.

'To Flag-Officer-in-Charge Hull ... from HMS *Rattlesnake* ... Sailed in accordance with your 0910 stroke ... er eighty-four, stroke ten.' He hesitated and looked across at Turner busily scratching at his pad, his fingers already red with the icy cold. But Bunts did not look up. The fact gave him confidence. 'No further apologies – wish me luck.'

Turner dutifully scribbled down the rest of the message while Andrews wondered whether he had gone too far. After all the man was an admiral. 'Oh, why not worry about that in a month's time when we come back to port?' he told himself doubtfully, as Bunts started to stow away his pad.

'Is that all, sir?'

'Yes.' Then the old fear at his own boldness overcame him. 'One thing, better make sure it gets into the hands of the admiral himself. Direct it to Vice-Admiral Fox-Talbot, DSC.'

Turner's mouth dropped open and he

looked at the captain, as if the officer had just insulted his mother.

'What's the matter, Turner?' Andrews snapped. 'Didn't you hear?'

'I heard all right, sir,' Turner said, recovering himself. Quickly he scribbled down the words, hardly knowing how he managed to get them down. 'Vice-Admiral *Fox*-Talbot, DSC.'

He staggered blindly down the companionway towards Erickson's bunk to tell him the terrible news, while up on the little bridge Lieutenant Andrew Andrews stared at the darkening clouds ahead and told himself he was going to war at last.

DAY TWO: DECEMBER 23rd, 1941

'It is our duty to ensure that not one drop of petrol or one British-made bullet reaches the Reds.'

Admiral Doenitz, Head of the U-Boat Service, 1941.

'Stillgastanden!'

The big dockside shed, open at three sides, echoed and re-echoed with the crash of their jackboots. One hundred and sixty officers and men, the crews of four U-boats, snapped to attention in unison, as if they were still at the submarine training school in Müwik. 'St Pauli Willi,' Kapitänleutnant Schulze, the senior captain who had gained his nickname because he insisted that every one of his crew join him in the Hamburg St Pauli brothels at the end of each cruise, swung round and threw Doenitz, what Hartmann could not help thinking, was the father of all salutes.

Outside, the December wind blustered across the fiord and rippled the waters of

Kiel Harbour into a series of white-topped breakers, which rocked the mine-sweepers, lying aft of the U-boats, back and forth with monotonous regularity.

Doenitz acknowledged the salute with a curt, *'Danke, Herr Kapitänleutnant'*, and then followed by sallow-faced, little captain von Friedeburg, along with the rest of the smartly uniformed golden pheasants and his adjutants, the 'Big Lion', as the U-boat men called him behind his back, passed down the ranks of the crews. Here and there he paused and asked a question or commented on a new decoration one of the 'Lords' was wearing, his keen blue eyes scanning each and every face.

Finally he was satisfied and climbed stiffly on the trolley, while the Party Officials, whose elaborate uniforms had gained for them the nickname of golden pheasants grouped themselves around him officiously. The Big Lion nodded towards St Pauli Willi, who swung round and bellowed at the top of his voice as if he were an army drill instructor, rather than a skilled U-boat captain who had learned his trade with Prien, Kretschmar and the rest:

'Parade – *parade, stand at ease!*'

The 'Lords' did so gratefully. They had

been waiting in the freezing shed for over an hour before Admiral Doenitz and his entourage had appeared. They shuffled their feet rapidly to get the lift back in them and then settled down to hear what the Head of the U-boat Weapon had to say to them. Out of the corner of his eyes Leutnant Heiko Hartmann took a quick glance at his own men to check that they were behaving themselves. They were. The few weeks back in port had done them a world of good. The beards were gone and the colour had returned to their strained faces. In their smart blue uniforms with the jaunty beribboned caps (instead of the usual salt-stained leather jackets and sidehats) they looked like peacetime sailors, who had all the time in the world to devote to their appearance.

'Germans! ... Comrades!' Doenitz's thin high voice came from the loudspeakers and drowned the shrill scream of the gulls outside. 'I will not waste words. Soon you will be running out to fight the enemy once again. Up to this summer the battle you fought was against an enemy – the British – who were courageous, tough and obstinate. And you were winning that battle. Now a new enemy has joined that battle – the Soviet monster. But in spite of his size, he is not to be feared. Our brave comrades of the Army are forcing their way to Moscow step by step and there is no doubt that soon they will be victorious there. Still we have a role – a major role – to play in that land battle too. It is our duty to ensure that not one drop of petrol or one British-made bullet reaches the Reds.'

Admiral Doenitz looked around at their blue-clad ranks challengingly and Hartmann could not help thinking what an inspiring leader the 'Big Lion' was. He knew his submarines and his submariners – after all he had been a U-boat commandant himself in World War One before the Tommies had sunk him, and he had one son in the same branch in this war too. He talked the language the 'Lords' understood.

'Some of you are new to the service,' Doenitz continued. 'Others of you have been out before and know the dangers. But both groups must realize the vital task before you when you leave here.' The Admiral's voice rose above the sudden clank of a winch over at the Howaldt Ship Works beyond the fiord. 'When you return from your next mission, comrades, the boys among you will come back men – and the men will be heroes!'

Hartmann felt a thrill of emotion run

through his well-trained body, punished by years of rigorous training in the Hitler Youth, the Work Service and now the Navy. The 'Big Lion' spoke the very words he felt in his own heart. This time he would take the U-122 out and return a hero. He must.

He had been in the Kriegsmarine for five years now, and it had taken him all that time to get his own ship. In that same period of time his father had been given command of an infantry division which was even now fighting outside the gates of Moscow. Klaus, his brother, was already a lieutenant-colonel in the Luftwaffe. And although it had cost him a leg to do so, he did have his own wing and had cured his 'throatache' to boot.

His fellow commanders in the pack had also relieved themselves of the same complaint and the coveted Knight's Cross of the Iron Cross hung round all their necks. As the Training School Band for Mürwik struck up the Submariners' Song, Heiko Hartmann clenched his fists and swore a solemn oath to himself that he would sink more enemy tonnage this trip than any other commander in the pack.

Suddenly the band faltered and broke off playing. Hartmann tore his mind away from his own problems. One of the Admiral's adjutants had come running across the wet dockside and was whispering urgently to Captain von Friedeburg, while the 'Big Lion' stared down at the two of them with ill-concealed impatience and the golden pheasants glanced at each other inquiringly.

Finally von Friedeburg hurried up the steps and muttered a few hasty words to Doenitz. The 'Big Lion' nodded, his hard face revealing nothing. Then he stepped to the microphone. Once more his high-pitched voice echoed throughout the big shed.

'Comrades, I have just received exciting new information from our air intelligence. It is news that could ensure every one of you – even the rawest Moses,' he meant the youngest member of the crew, 'getting a piece of tin!'

A barrel-chested Obermaat from 'St Pauli Willi's' crew stepped forward, pulled off his beribboned cap with his big red fist and yelled enthusiastically:

'Three cheers for the Admiral! Hip, hip, hurrah!'

A great wave of cheering swept through the shed, a little hesitant at first, but gathering momentum, as the Obermaat shouted again, engulfing the thin figure standing on the platform. Flushed with pleasure, Admiral Doenitz held up his hands for silence.

'Thank you comrades,' he rasped. 'I was certain that the news would please you. But now we must work. Commanders will stand down their crews for–' he checked his watch swiftly '–for twelve hours, while new operational plans are worked out.' Brushing aside the usual formalities, he took over the parade himself. 'Commanders will report to me immediately after the parade is dismissed. Now – watch your front!' His voice rose. *'Attention!'*

As Hartmann clicked stiffly to attention with the rest of his crew he told himself that this was the first time he had ever been drilled by an admiral; there really must be something big in the wind.

'Gentlemen, your attention please,' Captain von Friedeburg snapped. The four U-boat commanders put down their glasses of grog, which Kapitänleutnant Sobe had offered them as soon as they had come aboard the depot ship *Hamburg*. The steaming hot rum and water had been just what they had needed after the icy cold of the parade, but the Big Lion had declined the flotilla captain's offer. He had gone immediately to the map room. Now obviously he was ready for them. Obediently they followed von Friedeburg into the big cabin where he was waiting for them, Schulze in front, as protocol prescribed, and Hartmann bringing up the rear.

'Beg to report present, sir!' Schulze snapped.

'Stand at ease, Schulze,' the Big Lion said impatiently.

Hartmann could see the Big Lion's eyes were gleaming. Obviously he couldn't wait to tell them his news.

'All right, gentlemen, this is it. The Tommies are going to have another go at getting through to Murmansk!'

An excited gasp rose from the young skippers, but Doenitz stopped it immediately with his raised hand.

'Yes, even after their last defeat, they are going to try to get a convoy through. One of our Luftwaffe chaps spotted a convoy leaving the Humber yesterday. Unfortunately he was shot down, but he did alarm his own people. Early morning air reconnaissance by the dead chap's comrades from Holland confirmed his report. About thirty ships heading due north.' He rapped the big map spread out on the table in front of him. 'Their destination is obvious: Russia. And, gentlemen, I don't need to tell you, I think, that we of the U-boat Weapon are going to get the lion's share of stopping them. After all, the men don't call me the Big Lion for nothing, do they?' He allowed himself a thin smile, while the young captains laughed; so the old man knew about his nickname too. He seemed to have his eyes and ears everywhere.

'What about the Fifth Air Fleet, sir?' asked Hansen of the U-33, who, for some obscure reason, insisted on wearing the wing collar of the Imperial Navy. 'They'll try to get in first, won't they? Those Luftwaffe boys will surely feel that this convoy is their own special pigeon. After all they did spot it first, sir.'

'No doubt, Hansen. I am quite certain that Reichsmarshal Goering's air staff is working on that very problem at this moment – at top speed.' Doenitz sniffed disdainfully. 'However, the aeroplane is meant for the air and the ship for the sea. The water and everything that floats on it are the concern of the Kriegsmarine. In short, that Tommy convoy is ours and I intend to see that your group, Schulze, get the kudos for sinking this one – and the subsequent glory.' He paused and looked at

St Pauli Willi significantly.

Hartmann, standing to Schulze's left, allowed himself a delightful few seconds thinking of all that meant: the special radio bulletin from Berlin, the girls with the flowers and the bands to welcome them when they sailed back into Kiel Harbour, the triumphant tour of the war factories, perhaps even a reception by the Führer himself, and above all that most coveted piece of 'tin' – the Knight's Cross or the Iron Cross. Then Doenitz was speaking again and he dragged himself back to the present.

'My guess is that the Tommies' tactics won't change from the last convoy – the British are a conservative people, mentally lazy. They will go to Iceland as usual to be joined by their escorts coming up from Seydisfiord. The heavy stuff will cover them till they reach Bear Island. My guess is, however, that they won't go beyond the Island or the longitude of North Cape – twenty-five degrees east.' He stabbed the map with a long forefinger. 'After all they will reason there will not be any danger of an attack from one of our surface raiders and therefore dispense with the heavier escorts. From this point onwards the Tommies will rely on their close escorts, destroyers, frigates and the like, and whatever Bolshevik or Tommy submarines which are in the area. Now, gentlemen, the question is, where are we going to strike the convoy – before they pass into the Barents Sea or after? If we strike before they pass through – what I believe the Tommies call 'the gate' – into the Barents and White Sea, we may run into danger from the cruisers' air support. But – we might also have an opportunity to sink one of those cruisers, a delightful possibility. If we strike *after* they have passed through the gate, there is the problem of the Fifth Air Fleet.' He paused. 'Do I have to say more?'

Doenitz did not. It was obvious to the young U-boat captains what he meant. The closer the convoy came to Russia, the more opportunity the Luftwaffe had of launching air strike after air strike against the convoy and thus gaining the victory for themselves.

The Big Lion looked at Hartmann, his most junior captain.

'The Tommies like to pride themselves on being the Senior Service,' he said with a thin smile on his lips as he examined the youngster's keen, chiselled face with the aggressive blue-grey eyes. 'We of the Kriegsmarine do not worry about such things. Let us not stand on ceremony therefore; let us ask our Moses here what he would do?'

Hartmann licked his suddenly dry lips. The others stared at the Moses, half amused by, half sympathetic towards his confusion. He began slowly, formulating his idea as he spoke.

'Well, sir, it's my guess that the Luftwaffe chaps will jump the gun. They'll know we'll be out there somewhere too. So they'll make their attack at the maximum possible range, just as the Tommies begin to come up to the Gate.' He paused for the Big Lion's approval.

'So, sir, if we were waiting at that max range when the Fifth Air Fleet came in, we would stand the risk of being hit by our own bombs–'

'What do you mean?' Lothar the Locomotive interrupted. The fourth skipper who was called the 'locomotive' not because of his enormous size – he was much too big for the U-boat service – but because he had once actually torpedoed a locomotive chugging along some Aegean railway line.

Now he pulled a face. 'Those perfumed warm brothers of the Luftwaffe couldn't even slap their own mother sitting opposite them!'

Hartmann smiled faintly.

'Maybe. But as I was saying, we would risk the danger of being bombed by our own people, although at the same time, the Fifth boys would do the job of scattering the convoy for us – including the heavy escort vessels. After that, we'd–' he stopped abruptly, realizing that his fellow captains fully understood what he meant.

'A capital idea, Hartmann!' Doenitz exclaimed with unusual emotion. He turned to the others. 'You see, gentlemen, Moses is much smarter than we think. Out of the mouths of babes and sucklings, eh!' His smile vanished. 'All right, then, supposing we buy Hartmann's idea, how are we going to do it?' He bent over the map. 'My suggestion gentlemen, is that we should proceed like this...'

As the ships' sirens over at the Howaldt Works began to scream to the world that yet another 'grey wolf' had been launched the young captains bent over their charts.

Hartmann clattered up the stairs towards her apartment, not giving a damn whether Frau Lutz on the second floor heard him or not. He pressed the bell marked *Frau Kapitänleutnant Eva Carlson*, with the new note behind it 'widowed'. His heart was beating frantically, his breath coming in short, hectic gasps after the long run through the blacked-out streets. Eva opened the door herself, pale and very blonde in her simple black widow's dress, but appetizingly attractive.

'My God,' she gasped. 'I thought you'd sailed–'

He didn't give her time to finish. With a push he was past her and had pulled the door closed behind him.

'Postponed twelve hours,' he exclaimed, fighting to regain his breath. 'I've got two hours twenty ... before I have to report back...' He ripped at his jacket, slipping off his muddy shoes at the same time, oblivious to the mess he was making of her carpet. 'Come on, let's get to bed!'

'But we can't go to bed *now,*' she cried. 'It's only seven in the evening! Besides that old cow Lutz would be up against the wall with the glass to it, listening! You know what a busybody she is!'

He grabbed her by the arm and tugged her towards the bedroom.

'Who cares? I hope she gets a thrill out of it!'

For a moment her eyes rested on the black-draped photograph of her husband taken at

Laboe just before his last cruise; then she gave in to his urgent pleas and began to take her clothes off, folding them neatly on the chair until he knocked the underskirt out of her hand and commanded:

'We haven't time for that, Eva! I want you – and I want you damn quick!'

Afterwards she let him sleep a few moments, his blond head, sticky with sweat, pressed against her breast. She looked down at him tenderly. He seemed so young. Her husband had always looked so frighteningly fierce afterwards. She ran her pale hand gently across his face. He woke at once and ran his tongue round his dry lips.

'What time is it?' he asked.

She told herself that men were always concerned with time, as if it were running away from them at a gallop, but she didn't tell him that.

'You've got thirty minutes left,' she said softly and stroked his face once again.

He brushed it away and sat up.

'That was good, Eva,' he said, as if he had just eaten one of those sour roast and red cabbage dinners that her husband had always demanded when he had come home from a wartime cruise. 'I enjoyed that, I really did.' He pressed her thin hand absently. 'You are good to me – very good.' Without even a change of tone, he added: 'Give me a cancer stick will you, darling?'

Obediently she reached out to the cigarette box on the dressing-table, watching his face in the big mirror as she did so. It was a face that she had seen many times in these last two terrible years: first that of her dead husband, and then that of the other U-boat skippers who had sneaked into her bed after he had been posted missing. Drunken or solemn, desperate or calm, fanatic or cynic: each had the haunted look of men facing sudden death.

Leutnant Hartmann took a last glance at the Kiel Fiord. Then spitting over the side of the conning tower for luck, he clattered down the iron ladder in his seaboots. He knew that when he returned, the far bank would be lined with cheering crowds and not a few ragged Kiel whores screaming last greetings to their 'Lords'.

He dropped into the metallic world of the submarine's control area, already stinking of diesel and human sweat. Automatically he began to rap out the orders that he could now give – and sometimes did – in his sleep. Almost instantaneously the petty officers rapped back their replies:

'Foreship on diving stations … Midship diving stations … after-ship on diving stations.'

Above him the hatch cover dropped into place with a thud of finality. He checked whether the exhaust valves were closed, remembering his old instructor's terrible story of the fate of the old U-3 in Heikendorf Bay when the captain forgot to close the air inlet valves. They were.

'Prepare to flood tanks,' he ordered. Behind him the electric motors went into action and he could feel his ears begin to pop with the pressure change.

'Tanks ready,' Obermaat Duvendag snapped.

'Flood tanks!'

Behind him four ratings knelt and wrenched at the air levers. There was a sudden hissing noise. Air began to escape rapidly. Despite the fact that he had done this scores of times in the past, Hartmann's heart started to race at the thought of the danger now, as the water gurgled into the tanks.

The U-122 rocked gently forward and then backwards. A couple of moments and the boat righted itself. It was absolutely still save for the steady hum of the electric motors. Even the Moses, a nervous seventeen year old officer-cadet, knew that it was as much as his miserable life was worth to make a noise at this particular moment. In the corner the ratings worked feverishly at the hydroplanes, beads of sweat already beginning to form on their brows, spinning the large hand-wheels round as if they were grinding coffee.

'Sir!' a sudden cry rang the length of the ship.

Hartmann turned, startled. Who had broken the compulsory silence? An anxious sweating face was peering at him from the torpedo hatch.

'Sir – the fish has broken loose!'

'Take over, Dietz!' Hartmann yelled at his Number Two Leutnant Hans Dietz, and ran forrard.

He gasped. One of their 'fish' – the torpedoes – had slipped backwards from its tube and was protruding into the hatch. Four ratings were trying to push it back desperately, muscles rippling down the backs of their shirts already greasy with sweat, their breath coming in short hectic gasps. And they were failing. The U-122 only needed to move a couple of degrees and the fish would slip into the hatch and rip his ship to pieces.

Hartmann acted swiftly. He rushed the length of the boat.

'Dietz, fish sliding backwards!' he roared.

Even before Dietz could rap out his orders, the men on the hydroplanes began racing their big wheels round.

'You!' Hartmann yelled to the only unoccupied member of the crew, the seventeen year officer-cadet, 'follow me – at the double!'

Together they raced back forrard. Hartmann put his shoulder to the massive weapon and heaved.

'Heaven, arse and twine, man!' he bellowed at the deathly-pale cadet, 'give a hand, man!'... 'Now altogether, heave!'

As the U-122 began to settle on even keel under Dietz's expert guidance, the fish slid slowly back into its tube. The Petty Officer in charge quickly snapped the lock behind it, and stood before his captain, dripping with sweat, his hands trembling violently.

'Pull yourself together man!' Hartmann cried, wiping the sweat off his brow. 'What happened?'

The little PO, a Hamburger and a veteran of the Submarine Service, said hesitantly:

'I don't rightly know, captain ... I checked and locked the torpedo...' He looked around the little group of tense and sweating 'Lords', as if he hoped that one of them might help; but no one did. 'Perhaps a bolt jammed.'

'There's no goddam perhaps about it! You reported the diving all clear prematurely, didn't you!'

The veteran lowered his gaze.

'Yes ... yes, sir!'

For the next minute Hartmann 'made a sow' of the crimson-faced PO amazing himself with the number of his brother's eloquent Luftwaffe curse words he could remember. Finally he paused for breath and added more calmly. 'After all, Petty Officer, I suppose the Submarine Service is no old age insurance scheme, is it?' He forced a tight smile. 'Carry on, please.'

For the first time the veteran raised his eyes.

'Sorry, sir,' he mumbled. 'I promise you, it won't happen again.'

Hartmann knew it wouldn't; the Petty Officer would rather die from now onwards than let him down again. All the same when he was forced to go to the 'thunderbox' a few minutes later, he found out that when he reached for the hand-pump, his hand was trembling violently. It had been a close call – a very close call. As he began the hard job of pumping away the waste at a depth of twenty metres, he told himself grimly that if he were to gain that coveted piece of 'tin', there would have to be no more accidents in the U-122.

Hartmann wiped the lenses of his binoculars free with a piece of rag and stared once again the length of the U-boat at the horizon beyond the white spray of the bow. Below him the engines were pounding steadily. By now they must have made up for the time they had lost with the torpedo; the rest of the pack must be around somewhere.

Overhead, there were a number of long breaks in the dark clouds through which he could see the pale, silver glow of the stars. But when he peered ahead through his glasses it looked as if the U-122 was ploughing through a thick cloud of steam; then the icy stream of bow spray covered the lenses of the binoculars almost immediately.

He lowered them and checked if the look-outs crowding the conning tower with him were on their toes and alert. Feet spread apart against the roll of the waves, their hands clenched in enormous, thick mittens they were sweeping their prescribed arcs dutifully, peering through their binoculars as if their lives depended upon it. And in a way they did. For soon they would be entering the minefields that the RAF had laid across the exit into the North Sea. There were fairly well defined lanes through them, cleared by the men of the mine-sweeper flotillas. Yet there was always the danger that a lone RAF Sunderland flying-boat had sneaked in during the night and dropped another batch in the cleared lane.

'Nigger sweat, sir – a cup of nigger sweat?'

Hartmann turned round. It was the Torpedo PO, a steaming hot cup of coffee in his hand.

'Thought you might like this, sir. And Leutnant Dietz told me to tell you, sir, that we're approaching the minefield.'

'Thank you, Petty Officer.'

Hartmann smiled thinly as he tasted the burning black brew that contained more chicory than coffee. He must really have won the PO's heart if he were prepared to bring him coffee and run the risk of having his leg pulled as a 'brown-noser' by the rest of the crew.

The voice-pipe sounded. Hastily Hartmann flung the rest of the coffee overboard and dropped the cup. He picked up the tube.

'Yes?'

'We're in the field now, sir,' Dietz answered. 'And there's one of our boats ahead of us ... Zero-eight-five.'

'Thank you, Dietz.'

Hartmann focused his binoculars, bracing his legs against the swaying of the U-boat. They were fogged up almost immediately by the icy spray. He cursed, rubbed the lenses clear with his rag and focused them again. Then he spotted it – a lean grey shape against the horizon, perhaps five or six hundred metres away and a little to starboard. He picked up the voice-pipe.

'Dietz? Whose ship is that?'

'I think Lothar the Locomotive's – Captain Krueger's, sir.'

'Good. Well, I want you to take a bearing on him and follow him at this distance.'

'Ay ay, sir.'

A few moments later the U-122 swung a little to starboard and began to plough along in the wake of the other boat, rocking slightly as it hit the waves thrown up by Krueger's U-87.

An hour went by. Although it would soon be dawn, there was no sign of the sky beginning to break up yet. A new watch came up on the tower, but Hartmann did not go down with the old watch. Even though he had been up there for six hours now, he did not feel tired. He accepted another cup of 'nigger's sweat', while the men of the new watch took off the darkened glasses which had accustomed them to the change from the naked harsh light of the submarine to the blackness outside.

Suddenly he heard the sound he had been dreading ever since they had entered the minefield. A rusty scraping along the hull.

'Dead slow!' he ordered immediately.

Dietz reacted swiftly. The U-122 lost speed. On the conning-tower the new watch tensed, their eyes directed on the grey heaving surface of the water. Nothing. But the rusty scraping sound did not stop. Hartmann licked his dry lips, his hands clenched tensely as they crept along in agonizing suspense. Ahead of them the U-87 had slowed down too. The new mines were everywhere. He heard a sudden blow on the metal. Hartmann held his breath. *Was this it?* He could feel a cold trickle of sweat down the small of his spine.

'There she is, sir!' one of the new watch cried out. 'Over there!' A dark horned globe was bobbing on the surface of the water. A mine. Obviously they had just cut its cable. Hartmann breathed out hard; they were lucky to have survived.

'Full ahead, Dietz,' he snapped. 'Close up on Lothar the Locomotive!'

Hartmann could hear the junior officer's sharp intake of breath.

'Do you hear me?' he called.

'Ay ay, sir.'

Below, Dietz gave his orders and the diesels started to hum loud again as the U-122 picked up speed. Ahead the U-87 was still at dead slow. They closed quickly and Hartmann could make out the other boat's details quite clearly, the cluster of look-outs staring curiously at the U-122. Hartmann ignored the stares. Lothar the Locomotive dared not break radio silence to warn him off. When they had returned to base, he would admit to Lothar the trick he had played and the other captain would laugh and say he was a cunning dog, because there would be nothing else he could say. And if Lothar did not return, well–

The minutes passed leadenly while the two U-boats crept forward one behind the other. Now Hartmann felt perfectly calm. In a flat voice, he declared:

'These minefields are overrated. Especially if you can find some other mug to do the dirty work for you.' He indicated the U-87.

One or two of the watch laughed drily, but most of them were too keyed up to appreciate either his humour or his cunning.

'Not much more now, sir,' Dietz said over the voice-pipe. 'According to the chart we're about through. Unless those shitty Tommies have plastered the whole area with new mines.'

'Thank you, Dietz. No, I don't think they could have–'

Hartmann's words were drowned by a roar as the U-87 hit the mine. As the bright flame leapt into the night sky, the U-122 shuddered violently. Shaking his head to clear it from the shock of the blast, Hartmann saw that the U-87 was sinking rapidly. Its conning-tower was tilted at an impossible forty-five degree angle. Men were diving rapidly into the water, their shapes stark against the leaping flames.

'Shall we stand by, sir?' the officer-cadet called.

Hartmann did not reply. In the water the little red lights on the submariners' lifebelts were flicking on automatically as the U-87 started its last dive with a rending sound that carried clearly over the silent water.

'Stand by for what?' said Hartmann finally.

The officer-cadet looked at him as if he had gone mad.

'Why – to pick up the survivors, sir!' he stammered.

Behind the boy, the wizened PO had picked up the flare-pistol, ready to fire a cartridge and illuminate the scene.

'Put that down, Petty Officer,' Hartmann rapped.

'Sir,' the officer-cadet said, 'the survivors!'

With a strange sucking sound that diverted their whole attention for a moment, the U-87, with 63,000 tons of enemy shipping and one locomotive to its credit, disappeared beneath the waves. The little red lights began to move faster as they tried to escape the suction.

'Swim for Chrissake!' a member of the watch screamed at the red lights in a frenzy. *'Swim!'*

'Stop that!' Hartmann said harshly. 'No more of that shouting.'

But the cadet was not to be silenced. 'Aren't we going to rescue them, sir?' he asked plaintively.

Hartmann swung round on him as the red lights drifted closer.

'Of course, we're not going to rescue them,' he hissed. 'What kind of fool are you, to think we're going to heave to now? Look at that sky. It'll be dawn in a matter of minutes and – we'll be here like sitting ducks just waiting for some crappy Tommy pilot to come along and knock us off at his leisure!' Hartmann glared at the cadet, gasping for breath. 'This is not the history books of naval warfare with noble deeds and gallant sailors – this is the real war! And you'd better understand it quickly, if you're going to survive out here!'

Hartmann swung round again. The sea was full of sudden flotsam ejected from the sunken submarine's open conning-tower: floats, bottles, what looked like a joint of beef, charts – and a dead man, suspended by a rubber lifebelt, face upwards, open eyes staring sightlessly into a merciless dawn. But it wasn't the debris or the dead man that Hartmann and the rest of the watch on the conning-tower saw as the U-122 began its terrifying progress through what was left of the U-87. It was survivors, now no longer just red lights in the water; but struggling, oil-drenched sailors, their panic transformed into hope as the U-122 cut through the gleaming oil slick all about them. Gasping and choking with the seawater, they reached up out of the slick and waved at the men up above them on the conning-tower, shouting, 'Over here, comrade … over here!'

Hartmann spotted one man, completely naked, his face black with oil, treading water, his teeth very white as he cried joyfully, 'And even the niggers in Africa shout, home to the Fatherland, home to the Fatherland!' As the conning-tower came parallel with him, he stared up at Hartmann and stretched out one arm as if to seize the rope that would be thrown down to him. The grin died on his black, oil-covered face.

'Hey, comrades,' he yelled, 'throw me a line!'

The men on the conning-tower stared down at him stonily. The survivor caught sight of the tarnished gold on Hartmann's cap and recognized him as the captain.

'Skipper,' he cried with renewed hope, as the swell from the U-122 began to strike him in the face, 'get those St Pauli pimps to sling me a rope!' He choked as a wave swamped him and his words ended with a sudden bout of coughing. He came up struggling frantically, as if he knew now that they were going to abandon him. 'Skipper, for God's sake, *skipper!*' he yelled as the U-122 swept by him. 'Don't leave me!...'

The rest of the survivors were beginning to realize the terrible truth. Their desperate cries for help came in from all sides.

'Mates, you've got to help us!... I've got a wife and two kids back in Barmbeck ... Hey, you Jonni Hespers, I know you ... We served together in the *Schleswig*... You can't do this to me – I'm not in the U-boat service ... I'm a paymaster...' Waving and shouting desperately, their white blobs of faces vanished into the black, heaving waste of water. They became blinking red lights once more, while the men on the conning-tower stared ahead in stony silence, broken only by the continuous, slowly receding cry of, 'Comrade ... *Comrade.*'

Thirty minutes later the sky began to flush with the first light of the false dawn. It was time to go below. Hartmann yawned lazily and took one last look at the heaving, wintery sea. It would be another twenty hours, perhaps, before he saw it again.

'All right,' he rapped, 'clear the conning-tower, prepare for diving!'

The watch needed no urging. They filed down the dripping wet steel ladder into the thick, oil-heavy atmosphere below, blinking as it bit into their eyes, but glad to escape into its warmth.

Hartmann watched them go and told himself that luck, aided by his own cunning, had been on his side that night. He spat over the tower to appease the gods and followed. As he fastened the hatch behind, automatically dodging the seawater which drained down on to his upturned face, he whispered to the shining blank metal plate:

'And that's the way it's going to stay, do you hear me?... Luck and cunning – that's the way I'm going to win my piece of tin on this trip...'

DAY THREE: DECEMBER 24th, 1941

'Nothing better than a little drop of Nelson's blood to put the heart into a man again after a shock, sir.'

CPO Thirsk to Lieutenant Andrews.

'Come back, come back, Jolly Jack Straw,' Sparks was reading out the *Ballad of Jack Overdue* in his plaintive East Yorkshire voice, following the poem with his dirty forefinger in the crumpled three-day old copy of the *Daily Mirror*, 'There's ice in the killer sea. Weather at base closes down for the night. And the ash-blonde WAAF is waiting tea–'

'Well, you can put a sock in that rubbish for a start,' Bunts cut in grumpily. 'What the hell do you call that, eh?'

Sparks looked across at him from his rumpled bunk, where he was lying with dirty grey blankets piled up high on top of him and the end of his red nose sticking out from a Balaclava, his hands clad in holed khaki mittens.

'It's a poem, Bunts,' he answered. 'It says

(December 22nd–31st, 1941)

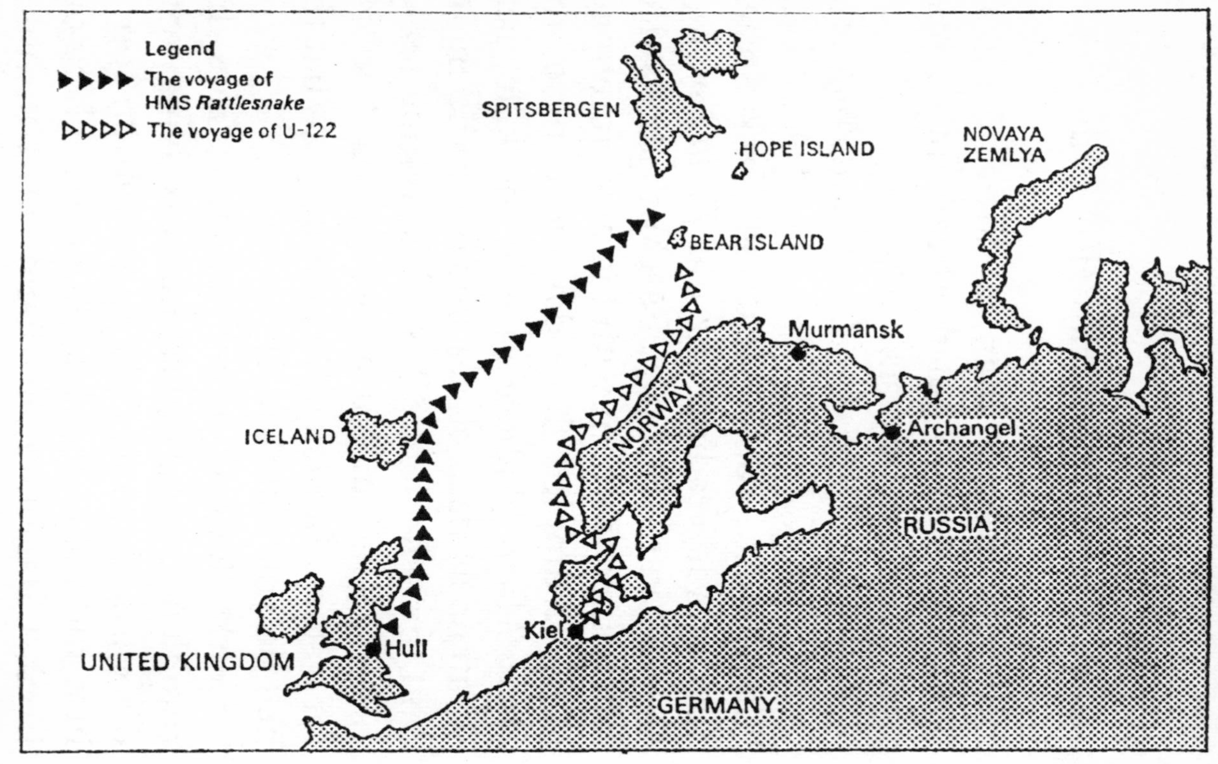

so in the *Mirror.*' He wiped the grey bead of dew at the end of his nose with the back of his mitten. 'What's up with you – ain't you got no culture? You went to the ABCA lectures back in training, didn't you?'

'Culture,' Bunts snorted. 'Course I have! I won the scripture prize when I was a kid in school in Brid. But that ain't no poem. Poems is supposed to rhyme, like them in the latrine. "It's no use standing on the seat, the crabs in this place jump six feet". That's poetry.' He hawked fiercely and spat on the dirty greasy metal deck. Another member of the standdown watch, sipping a mug of cocoa near the steaming kettle on top of the old pot-bellied stove, which was the crew's only form of heating, grumbled:

'Dirty bugger! Yer not at home in Hull, you know!'

Bunts ignored him.

'Besides,' he continued, 'who reads the *Mirror* except to look at them stupid letters from the brown jobs about the glasshouse – and to get a gander at Jane's tits... Has she got her knickers on in this one?'

Sparks did not get a chance to reply. Erickson's voice cut into the discussion from the head of the ladder which led into the crew's cramped quarters:

'And I'll have the knickers off'n you, Bunts, if you're not out of that pit right smartish!'

'But we've got to have our rest,' the man drinking cocoa protested. 'We only come off an hour ago.'

'Don't tell me,' Erickson snapped. 'Tell the captain. He'll be down here in a brace of shakes to have a look at how the other half lives.'

'Oh him,' Bunts said lazily and made an elaborate pretence of yawning. 'He's soft titty.'

Erickson looked at Bunts, who had served with him once before the war on the fishing boats.

'Ay that might be – he's not a bad bloke. But I thought I'd just tell you gentlemen of leisure that the CPO's with him.'

That did it. Thirsk might be a soft touch at times, but they also knew he was a stickler for discipline and orders; he hadn't been in the Royal for thirty years for nothing. With a grin on his face, Erickson watched how the off-duty crew jumped out of their bunks and began to tidy up the mess. A few moments later Erickson heard the hollow ring of the two of them descending the steep ladder into the hold, which now served as the crew's quarters.

'Stand by your bunks!' he snapped, standing as best he could in the confined rolling space. 'Captain's inspection.'

Lieutenant Andrews touched his cap in acknowledgement and said quietly:

'Please stand at ease.'

The crew relaxed, but their tired eyes were fixed on a ramrod-straight CPO Thirsk standing just behind the captain and eyeing the mess with obvious disgust.

For a moment or two Andrews examined the long narrow room, lined with bunks, lit by a naked electric light bulb and the ruddy glow from the gaps in the stove. The place stank of oil, stale sweat and the odour of damp metal. He wrinkled his nose up in disgust. His gaze fell on the mess-table which ran the length of the quarters. It was a confused wasteland of dirty mugs and plates from breakfast. A great seven pound issue tin of strawberry jam squatted in its centre, its lid roughly skewered open and stuck upwards like the petals of a monstrous flower.

'Hm,' he cleared his throat. But as usual he could not find the right words.

'The lads don't have any proper tools, sir,' CPO Thirsk explained. 'So everyone digs into everything with his pocket knife. That's why it looks a bit of a mess.'

Again Andrews could think of nothing else to say but 'hm'. Instead he walked closer to the table, where a loaf of bread, smeared with oily fingerprints had fallen into a pool of tea spilt on the table.

'A bit wasteful, isn't it?' he said at last, pointing to the bread. 'That's probably one of the last of the loaves. The cook's mate told me at breakfast that we are going on biscuits tomorrow.'

CPO Thirsk shot a fierce glance at Erickson; let him get the lazy bastards out of this one. Petty Officer Erickson understood the look and he rose to the occasion.

'Nothing'll be wasted, sir,' he said hastily. 'Sparks here's a great baker – aren't you, Sparks?'

Sparks, who had not even burned a piece of toast since his childhood, nodded.

'Yes, sir, I like baking, sir. Spend all me time at it when I'm home on leave.'

Behind Andrews' back, CPO Thirsk raised his eyes heavenwards.

'So,' Erickson continued, 'what he'll do with that bread is he'll add a few currants and make a bread pudding. He might even bake a little cake – jam sponge. We've got plenty of jam. You see–'

'All right, Erickson,' CPO Thirsk cut in. 'The Captain's heard enough of Sparks' talents in the kitchen.'

Andrews smiled hesitantly.

'What's that?' he indicated a line of galvanized iron basins, fixed into holes on a wooden table.

'That's the crew's ablutions, sir,' CPO Thirsk replied. 'And over here, sir, if you'll follow me.' Carefully he steered him away from the filthy table towards two cubicles located in the gloom at the back of the place. 'We've got the lavatories.'

Andrews pulled a face.

'Yes, I can smell it, Chief.'

'We try to keep 'em from freezing up, Sir. Every watch is supposed to put hot water down them when they're off duty.' He indicated the blackened kettle steaming on the stove. 'But the first thing most of them want when they come off watch is a cup of char or cocoa – and that's where the hot water goes.'

Andrews absorbed the information, staring at the myriad pencil drawings of women and men engaged in intricate sexual intercourse which decorated the latrine walls. His eyes fell on the scrawled couplet in red ink:

'This bloody roundhouse is no good at all. The seat's too high and the hole is too small.'

Below it another hand had written: 'To which I must add the obnoxious retort. Your arse is too large and your legs are too short!'

With all his strength, Lieutenant Andrews tried to fight back the smile which sprang to his lips. He failed and laughed out loud. CPO Thirsk shook his head and told himself yet again that the new skipper was nothing but an overgrown school lad, with the eggshell still stuck behind his lugs.

'Sir,' he barked, trying to save Andrews' dignity and authority in the eyes of the crew, 'If you'd care to follow me over here, I'll show you where we keep the spare ammo for the Oerlikon.'

'Thank you, Chief.'

But Lieutenant Andrews was not fated to see the spare ammunition for their main weapon that day. Just as he had turned to follow a stiff-legged Thirsk, a rating's face appeared at the head of the ladder.

'Sir,' he yelled. 'Sir, we've just spotted PQ 8!'

The snow had stopped now leaving the

ships starkly outlined against crisp, blue winter sky. As he and Thirsk swept their length through their glasses, Andrews could hear the men on gun-watch discussing the pros and cons of the tankers which seemed to make up the bulk of the convoy.

'You can keep the fancy grub and sheets on the beds,' a big Londoner named Hawkins was saying, 'Yer sitting on a bloody volcano on them things.'

'But they've got real cooks and real quarters,' a Hull man with a cock-eye protested. 'The Yanks even get pictures on theirs.'

'Yeah, and they have to crawl around in brothel-creepers in case the nails on yer boots cause a fire and yer can't even have a spit-and-a-draw on deck. No thanks, mate, you can have 'em.'

'That's a Blue Funnel boat, sir,' CPO Thirsk explained, still not lowering his binoculars. 'Used to be in the tea trade out East before the war... And that twin stack over there, that's the old Strickline. They was mostly in the Med and the Gulf in the old days and–' He broke off suddenly, finding at last what he had been searching for. Andrews caught his hastily suppressed gasp of pleasure and he glanced at the CPO out of the corner of his eye.

'What is it, Chief?' he asked.

'That's the *St George*, sir, the pride of the Ellerman Wilson Line.' He licked his lips, cracked and bloody from the keen wind. 'My son's fourth officer on her.'

Andrews took his gaze away from the sleek tanker loaded with the precious oil which would mean all the difference for the Russians fighting for their lives before Moscow.

'I didn't know that, Chief. I didn't know that you were old enough to have a son,' he added with a smile. 'Still it must be nice for you to have him along with us.'

'Yes, it is that, sir.' Thirsk thrust a gnarled knuckle into his eye. 'Ruddy wind really gives my eyes jip,' he said thickly.

Suddenly Lieutenant Andrews had a brilliant idea. 'Listen, Chief,' he said enthusiastically, 'why don't you send him a message?'

'But we couldn't do that, sir – could we?'

'Of course we can. But we've just got to make it look Navy, that's all. Get Bunts up here and we'll get it right off on the Aldis Lamp.'

Minutes later Lieutenant Andrews was dictating his message to Bunts.

'Very best wishes to the master of *St George*. Proverb 8, Verses 32–33.'

'If you'll forgive me, sir, but what does the last bit of the signal mean?' CPO Thirsk asked, when Bunts had passed the message.

The young captain proud of his ruse explained:

'Well, I was the pride of the local church before I went to boarding school. I learned a lot of the Bible by heart. I hope it means: And now, my sons, listen to me. Happy are those who keep my ways.'

Thirsk chuckled.

'He'll like that, sir,' he exclaimed, the tears springing to his old eyes again. 'He'll like that very much. Peter was always a one for a laugh. You can bet when we get back to Hull, we'll have many a good laugh about this one.'

Erickson never found out exactly when the little bastard joined the convoy. But as soon as the alarm bells started to sound on the nearest merchantman, he swung his glasses round to starboard and spotted him in the clear winter sky at three miles range. Dropping them hastily, he cupped his hands to his mouth and bellowed: *'Shad!'*

'Shad!' the cry was taken up everywhere.

The alarm began to jangle. The off-duty men poured up from below, struggling into their duffle-coats, pulling on their steel helmets, crying out for information. Roughly Erickson pushed his way through them and caught the skipper as he emerged from his cabin, his face still drugged with sleep.

'Sir,' he rapped.

'Yes,' Andrews replied, fumbling with his steel helmet. 'What is it?'

'A Shad, sir!'

'A what?'

'A shadow, sir. Sorry. We call 'em Shads. It looked to me like a Blohm and Voss 138 – over there to starboard.'

Andrews hastily focused his glasses and picked the seaplane up.

'I can see it now. What's the drill?'

'We stand to, sir. But if my experience is any value, sir, I wouldn't put everybody on the guns just yet. That 138 is just a Shad. He'll keep out of range until the Jerries in Norway start sending out the bombers. By that time the lads'll be worn out if we keep them all on stand-to.'

Andrews ran his mind quickly over their armament. There were the two Oerlikons on the bridge wings, twin Brownings on the 'monkey island' behind it and the two PAC rockets, which fired wires attached to rockets high into the air so that the enemy plane would entangle itself in the wire when it came in on a dive-bombing raid.

'All right on ruddy sparrows', he'd heard naval gunners grumble about them, 'weak sparrows!'

'You're right, Erickson. Thanks for the tip. Tell the Oerlikons to stand watch. The rest can stand down again for the time being. But I want everyone on his toes. They'll be more Jerries, as you say.'

'Too bloody true, mate,' Erickson growled to himself. But he did not tell the officer that. 'Ay, ay, sir,' he snapped, and hurried off to carry out the Captain's instructions.

The afternoon passed leadenly as the alerted convoy steamed due north. The first Shad was replaced by another, a Focke-Wulf Condor. With monotonous regularity, it circled the ships below, hour after hour until some German-speaking destroyer captain blinked out: 'Can't you please fly round the other way? You're making us dizzy.'

Still well out of range of their guns, the pilot of the four-engined reconnaissance-bomber signalled back cheekily.

'Anything to oblige an Englishman.' Moments later he broke off to starboard, made a lazy circle – and started to fly round them the other way.

The cold began to harden now, gripping their bodies with its icy fingers. The wind rose, shrieking in from the Arctic, penetrating their heavy layers of clothing as if they were mere sheets of paper. Flurries of snow followed.

Stamping up and down at the Oerlikons, the gunners, clad in battle-blouses, lambs-wool jerkins, greatcoats and duffle-coats, cursed and watched the Shad.

'If we only had a carrier,' Sparks grumbled to Erickson, who was now in charge of the gun crews, 'just a sodding little Woolworth would do.* He'd knock that bastard out of the sky in a brace of shakes.'

'Yeah,' Erickson said good-humouredly, 'and if me Aunt Fanny had a moustache, she'd be me Uncle Joe. You'll just have to grin and bear it, Sparks.' He tugged at the end of his nose a couple of times to get the circulation working again in case of frostbite. 'After the war, they'll give you a

*A type of mini-carrier, consisting of a converted merchantman carrying a dozen or so aircraft.

putty medal for all this.'

'Not us,' Bunts said sourly. 'Them Brylcreem lads in the RAF'll get all the gongs. They'll be the heroes, while we're back unloading sodding kits in Grimsby.'

'Talking of medals, did you hear the one about the RAF bloke who went up to the Palace to get his gong from the King?' Sparks said.

'No, and even if I had, you'd tell us it anyway,' Erickson said. 'Get on with it, Sparks.'

'Well, when this bloke gets up in front of the King – and you know how he stutters – the King asks him, "Didn't you shoot down a F-f-focke-Wulf to get this?"

'And the RAF bloke answers. "No it were two Focke-Wulfs, sir."

'So the King says, "never mind, Flight Lieutenant, you're only gonna get one f-f-fockin' medal!"'

Standing on the bridge, listening to them, Lieutenant Andrews laughed to himself, glad of the break from the leaden monotony of their progress and the threat which hung over them. He stamped over to the window feeling like a walking clothes store; for the first time in his life he was wearing the long woollen underpants which had been given him by the solicitous CPO Thirsk, who for some reason known only to him, called them John L Sullivans. Standing there swaying slightly with the swell, he focused his glasses on the Shad.

Over the convoy, the Aurora Borealis was beginning to flicker, its streamers dancing like cold flames, throwing an eerie glow over the ships steaming northwards at a steady seven knots. He tore his eyes away from its strange fascination and searched the luminous horizon until he found what he sought: the Condor, a sinister black spot in the limitless sky. Suddenly he caught his breath. The Shad was not alone. There was another evil black spot to his right. And another.

'Christ,' he cried to himself. 'Jerries!'

Adjusting the binoculars furiously, he concentrated on the horizon. Yes, there was no doubt about it. There were four or five enemy planes out there. He dropped the glasses and ran to the bridge door.

'Petty Officer Erickson!' he yelled. 'Sound the alarm! ... *Enemy planes!*'

As the alarm bells began to sound through the convoy, they came hurtling in low over the gleaming water, nine Junkers 88s, broken up into groups of three. Bright yellow-red started to flash along the destroyers' decks. A moment later came the explosions of their guns. The sky filled with soft black puffs of smoke. But the Junkers came on.

Rolling slightly from side to side, not more than a hundred feet above the water, they pressed home their attack at three hundred miles an hour. Suddenly they seemed to leap higher in the air. Black eggs began to tumble from their yellow painted shark-bellies.

Above the din of the ack-ack, Andrews could not hear the bombs' explosions, but he could see the huge pillars of ark-green water which swamped the closest merchantman. A moment later the planes roared over the HMS *Rattlesnake* like a flock of great blackbirds and Erickson's Oerlikons were peppering the sky furiously.

From all sides came the boom of the guns and the furious chatter of the machine-guns. The air was a crazy mess of glowing, zig-zagging tracer and exploding shells. It did not deter the German pilots. They came flashing in again to deliver their bombs from all directions. The seamen used to looking up at planes, now found themselves looking down at them as the Junkers came back at sea-level.

Then they had their first kill. Standing on the shell-littered Oerlikon platform behind the chattering gun, Andrews saw the nearest merchantman, the *Empire Durban,* was no longer steering a straight course, but was zig-zagging crazily out of control, badly hit.

The Junkers pressed home their advantage. Suddenly one of the yellow-bellied 88s roared over HMS *Rattlesnake,* almost touching the look-out in the top mast, and headed straight for the *Durban.* Furiously Sparks swung the Oerlikon round.

'Fire!' Erickson bellowed, above the roar of the plane's engines. Sparks pressed the foot pedal. The gun began to rock on its pedestal, as it poured a stream of white shells after the Junkers. Andrews could see the tracer curving off to the left. Sparks was giving too much aim-off.

'Right, Sparks! For Christ sake, *Right!*'

Sparks adjusted immediately. The tracer began to creep ever closer to the Junkers. And then suddenly the Oerlikon stopped its crazy frenzied chatter. Andrews swung round. The gun had jammed.

'You sodding idiot!' Erickson bellowed at Sparks who had immediately begun to struggle with the auto-loader. 'Don't you ruddy well know how to load a pig proper yet?' Roughly he pushed Sparks aside. 'Here, gimme that mask!'

But it was too late. As Andrews swung his glasses round again on the Junkers, he saw five black eggs detach themselves from her and strike the merchantman directly amidship. There was not even a moment of suspense. What happened next seemed like an episode in the cinema. Utterly detached, his world limited to the circle of the lenses, Andrews watched how the explosions were followed by a huge vomiting volcano, which shot thick black smoke and wreckage two hundred and fifty feet into the air. And then very slowly, the *Empire Durban* began to slide into the grey-green sea. Minutes later the Junkers were black spots on the horizon again.

'Sir.' It was the big Londoner Hawkins.

Andrews swung round.

'What do you want on the bridge?' he snapped. Then he saw the deathly pale look on the other man's face. 'What is it, Hawkins?'

The Londoner opened his mouth. Automatically Andrews noted that he had a tooth missing at the front. But nothing came when he tried to speak, just a kind of throaty animal sound. CPO Thirsk, who had just seen to his relief that the *St George* had not been hit, strode stiff-legged over to the Captain.

'Hawkins,' he said, 'answer when the captain asks you a question! Come on now, man, get it out!'

Again the rating opened his mouth, but all he could produce was the same animal grunt, his eyes wide with shock. He had the same look that Andrews remembered on an elderly school-teacher's face after she had been dug out of the rubble of her bombed home in 1940. He licked his lips helplessly and wondered what he should do. Thirsk was quicker off the mark. He raised his gloved hand and slapped Hawkins lightly across the face.

Hawkins shook his head, as if he were trying to wake himself from a deep sleep.

'Sir,' he stuttered thickly, 'the look-out...'

'What's the matter with the look-out?' Andrews snapped.

Hawkins held out his bemittened hand. The palm was stained a dark russet. Andrews looked down at it uncertainly.

'What is it?'

CPO Thirsk reacted first again.

'The look-out, sir,' he cried. 'He's been

hit. Come on, sir!'

But they were too late. Perched high above their heads, his riddled body slumped against the side of the cage, the look-out was already dead, the steady drip-drip of his blood on the heaving deck below, the only indication that he had once been alive.

Andrews fought back the bile that threatened to choke him and closed his eyes for a moment; the man was the first dead person he had ever seen in his whole life.

'I'll take care of it, sir,' Thirsk said gently. 'He must have caught a burst from that ruddy Junkers… He won't be very pretty. Erickson, get somebody–'

'Thank you, Chief,' Andrews interrupted, his voice thick and unrecognisable, 'I'll see to it.' Without looking at him, he said: 'Erickson, get someone to shin up the ladder and get him down. And ask somebody else to get a canvas sack and the ensign.'

By effort of will, Lieutenant Andrew Andrews forced himself to stare upwards at the dead look-out, while all around him the ratings waited in a heavy silence, broken only by the whistle of the wind and the steady drip-drip of the blood on the deck.

'Rum-O, sir,' Thirsk's voice came cheerfully

from beyond the heavy black-out curtain. 'Can I come in, sir?'

'Yes, come on in, Chief.'

The CPO pushed aside the blackout curtain with his shoulder, his gnarled, arthritic fingers curled round two mugs of issue rum. He beamed down at the young officer who was sitting up, fully clothed, on the rumpled bunk.

'I thought I'd take the liberty of bringing you a drop, sir, seeing it's a special occasion. The cook put a drop of hot water in it and some sugar, though–'

'Special occasion?' Andrews automatically accepted one of the chipped mugs, and indicated that Thirsk should seat himself.

'Thank you, sir. Well, sir, your first day in action.' Thirsk raised his mug. 'Here's to you!'

'Thank you,' Andrews sipped the fiery brew, realizing that it was the first time he had touched it in his two years in the Navy. During his short period in the lower deck, he had always swapped his daily ration with another rating for chocolate which he had sent home to his widowed mother in Eastbourne. Thirsk breathed out hard and wiped the back of his hand across his mouth.

'Nothing better than a little drop of

Nelson's blood to put the heart into a man again after a shock, sir,' he commented. 'I remember after Jutland I got the bosun's rope-end because I sneaked myself a nip while I was still under age.'

'Jutland!' Andrews exclaimed surprised. 'You were at Jutland?' The great World War One sea-battle was something he had read about in history books at school; he didn't think he'd ever talk to someone who had actually fought in it.

Thirsk's old face cracked into a tough grin.

'Yes sir, I was a boy seaman then – I'm not that old you know, sir. Though some of the lads in the crew think I was with Nelson!'

Andrews laughed.

'Do they?'

'Ay that they do, sir, when they've had a couple of ales in them and get a bit cheeky.' He took another sip of the rum and water.

'What's the drill now, Chief? How do we go from here?'

'Well, sir, if we're not lucky with the weather tomorrow – and Sparks tells me we're not going to be – old Jerry will be back in force, I have no doubt. And he'll keep plastering us all the way up to Bear Island. Though you never know in these latitudes and at this time of the year. The forecast might be wrong and we could be lucky enough to run into a snow-storm or a sudden fog.'

'But you don't think it's likely, do you Chief?'

'No, sir, it's bright as day outside and cold enough to freeze the goolies off'n brass monkey. Too cold for snow.'

'We might get a sudden front,' Andrews said sipping his rum and hating it.

'Past Bear Island, it's more likely. But that's another day and a half's sailing away. Up till then we'll just have to grin and bear it, sir.'

'And then?' he asked, finishing his drink.

'Then sir? Why then it's all plain sailing, apart from the ice-floes, the possibility that the Russkies drop their bombs on us by mistake – they don't seem to be much cop at ship recognition – and, of course, the Jerry subs.'

'All in all, Chief,' Andrews said 'it's going to be a very merry Christmas, isn't it?'

CPO Thirsk, just finishing his own drink, snapped the fingers of his free hand loudly.

'Oh ay, and that was the other thing, I was going to tell you, sir. The other special thing. I won't be on watch, when you come on in the morning, so I'd like to say on behalf of the lads and myself and Petty Officer Erickson – a Happy Christmas.'

'Happy Christmas?' echoed Andrews.

'That's right, sir,' Thirsk said happily, pulling up the collar of his greatcoat before facing the freezing night wind outside. 'It's Christmas Eve, you know, sir.'

Hartmann stared in silence at the vertical ebony mass towering five hundred metres above the white-capped sea. Everywhere else there was snow, ice – whiteness – but Bear Island was a desolate black. As the U-122 wallowed in the land swell, his first sight of the island reminded him of the time he had caught his first glimpse of the Eiger with the Hitler Youth, its bare, black north face rearing above thick snow of the *Bernse Oberland.* That, like this, made him think of the brutal tales of Nordic mythology.

Beside him on the conning-tower bridge, Dietz, buried in his leather and fur suit, shivered:

'God,' he shouted above the wind which came straight from the Arctic north, 'what a place! The arsehole of the world. Give me even Emden to this!'

Down below the off watch were still

celebrating their Christmas Eve dinner, veal cutlets, green cabbage, a cigar, a *Holsten Pils* and a small glass of *Doppelkorn.* Now the wizened Obermaat was attempting to squeeze *Auf der Reeperbahn nachts um half eins* out of his battered accordion and failing badly.

'This will be it, Dietz,' he shouted. 'Once the heavy escorts leave them, the Tommies'll scatter here as soon as the Fifth Air Fleet strikes them. Then it'll be every man for himself and we'll be waiting for them, picking them off at will.' He turned to the other officer, attempting to get some shelter from the freezing wind by bending his knees and crouching slightly. 'When does the Luftwaffe go in?'

'At dawn, sir. Or what goes for dawn in these latitudes in winter, sir. That's the word, at least, from HQ.'

Hartmann stared at Bear Island once more. Down below the Obermaat had given up on *Auf Der Reeperbahn* and had switched to *Stille Nacht, Heilige Nacht* with more success. Above the steady beat of the diesels and the roar of the wind, the Second Officer could catch the occasional snatch of the old Christmas carol.

'Funny, isn't it?' he said. 'Nearly a thousand

kilometres from nowhere and they still behave as if they were sitting back in some back street in Hamburg, celebrating the presentation* and the war did not even exist.'

'Sentimentality,' Hartmann answered, not taking his eyes off the black silhouette in front of him. 'Typical German sentimentality, petty-bourgeois and silly, not worthy of a great nation.'

'Oh, I don't know, sir,' Dietz said, trying to force a smile in the face of the wind. 'It's just an old carol, isn't it? It's something they remember from their childhood, inspired more by gin and beer than anything else.'

Hartmann remembered the past Christmases he had spent at sea, at first with the sea section of the Hitler Youth and then with the naval cadets. There had been no time for sentimentality on the great sail-driven training ship, just back-breaking work, starvation rations and brutal discipline. And he had been glad of it. Others had broken under the strain; he had thrived on it. That, too, was why he was the commander of the

*In Germany, Christmas presents are traditionally exchanged in front of the tree on Christmas Eve after a dinner and carol singing or poetry reading by the children.

U-122 and Dietz, who was only six months younger, was not. He was hard; Dietz wasn't.

He remembered the year before when he had been in Dietz's place serving as Kapitänleutnant Kraemer's first officer. They had sighted a British cargo ship out in mid-Atlantic, a fast new lease-and-lend vessel from the Amis, relying on its speed to get across without the protection of a convoy. It would have been the easiest thing in the world to have torpedoed her; but Kraemer was a sentimentalist just as Dietz was. He had insisted on surfacing and warning the British crew to abandon ship before finishing her off with the deck gun. Later, when the younger officer had protested about the obvious danger, he had lectured Hartmann that even in war 'one must obey the rules'.

'Remember, Hartmann,' he had said severely in his old-fashioned manner, 'the business of Christian seafaring doesn't cease because of a little thing like a war.'

Six months later when Hartmann had been posted back to Mürwick for another course, Kapitänleutnant Kraemer had done exactly the same thing and had been blasted out of the water by a couple of Tommy planes whose pilots knew nothing of the 'business of Christian seafaring'. When he had heard the news, Hartmann knew he had indirectly caused the loss of a valuable ship and forty odd highly trained men because he had not reported just what kind of sentimental fool Kraemer was. It was something that would not happen to him again.

There was a metallic clank of a hatch opening below. The boat's Moses, the young officer-cadet thrust his head through the top hatch and placed two steaming cups of black coffee on the wet deck. Easily he swung himself through and took up the cups again.

'Two cups of real gunfire,' he said cheerfully, slurring his words slightly so that Hartmann guessed he had been drinking with the off-duty watch. 'With the compliments of the Lords. They've put a good slug of *Korn* in them.'

Dietz accepted his gratefully.

'Just what I needed,' he cried, flipping back the top of the outer mitten so that he could hold the 'gunfire' with the silk glove below it. With an exaggerated gesture, parodying the typical Prussian army officer, he brought the mug up to the position of his third tunic button.

‘Captain – Horst,’ he barked, ‘may I take the liberty of wishing you both a happy and blessed Christmas Feast?’

Horst, the cadet, laughed exuberantly.

‘And a Happy Christmas to you gentlemen, as well!’

‘Happy Christmas,’ Hartmann echoed unenthusiastically, not even making a pretence of raising his mug: for Heiko Hartmann’s mind was not on Christmas, the feast of goodwill to all men. It was obsessed by the war and his desire for personal glory.

And asleep in his evil-smelling, dark, heaving cabin Andrew Andrews’ unconsciousness was preoccupied with other things as he tossed and turned in the narrow bunk. In his dream, he flung open the door of his mother’s dining-room and with a roar overturned the fine china cups of tea to the polite little screams of the old ladies who always came to their house in Eastbourne for tea on Sunday afternoons and special occasions like Christmas Eve. But the liquid which dripped out of the overturned cups on to the thick black carpet which was his mother’s pride was not tea, but blood.

DAY FOUR: DECEMBER 25th, 1941

'One wonders, ladies and gentlemen, how the sailormen of Convoy PQ 8 will be spending the festive season? My friends of the German Kriegsmarine tell me they are prepared to make it a warm, if wet one for them at least.'

Lord Haw-Haw, Deutschlandfunk,
Christmas Day, 1941.

Daylight came late. A few minutes afterwards the pale yellow sun peered over the grey horizon and lay there on the lip of the ocean, as if too feeble to rise any further. A few flurries of snow attempted to bar their way, turning the ships into grey ghosts; but they plodded on steadily, as if eager to attend their appointment with death. And the enemy came, as CPO Thirsk had predicted they would.

'Here they come!', they cried from ship to ship as the alarm gongs started to sound down the lanes. 'Happy sodding Christmas – here the bastards come!'

As the guns opened up in a sudden fury of flame and noise, Lieutenant Andrews caught sight of the first enemy attack formation skipping low over the white-topped surface of the water like a flight of water beetles on a pond.

'Heinkel 115s!' someone shouted on the Oerlikon deck.

Erickson, spreading cinders from the stove on the deck so that his crews wouldn't slip on the icy metal, dropped the shovel hastily.

'Torpedo planes, sir,' he yelled over his shoulder at Andrews. 'We'll have to be nippy on this one!' Before the big slow Hawkins could get to the starboard Oerlikon, he had pushed him roughly to one side and swung his tough body on to the gunner's seat.

'Stand by!' Andrews rapped at the helmsman and focused his glasses on the enemy planes. The Heinkel seaplanes were breaking up now and homing in on individual targets. But despite the sudden alarm, the merchantmen were keeping up an effective barrage. The deep boop-boop of their 'Chicago pianos' – banks of multiple machine-guns – mingled with the staccato bark of the escort's Bofors and Oerlikons. Suddenly the whole horizon was peppered a dark brown.

The barrage claimed its first victim. Through his glasses, Andrews saw one of the unwieldy seaplanes stagger as it took a long burst from a Chicago piano and a thin white stream of glycol begin to pour from one of its engines. Vindictively the other gunners concentrated on it. Tracer, red, white and green, stitched the grey sky, then the Heinkel's cockpit was a mass of flame. Andrews could see the pilot slumped across the controls behind the spider's web of shattered perspex. Leaving a fiery trail behind it, the seaplane hit the water with a tremendous splash, followed a second later by a blinding flash of exploding petrol. When it subsided, the Heinkel had gone. There was nothing left but a metal door slopping back and forth on the swell.

'Got the bastard!' the men of the *Rattlesnake* yelled exultantly. 'They've got him!'

But their triumph was shortlived. Although it seemed that nothing could live in that tremendous barrage, the Germans pressed home their attack. As Erickson opened up and the gun disappeared into a cloud of acrid black smoke with cork flying everywhere, the Heinkels started dropping their torpedoes. The sea was full of them, their trails criss-crossing the water everywhere as they sped towards their targets. The R/T burst into life all along the convoy lanes.

'Look out, *Nassau*, there's a fish heading straight for you! My Holy Christ, there's two coming at us!… Hard to port, Hull, for God's sake man – hard to port!' With the sweat pouring down their faces despite the icy cold, the merchantmen captains frantically spun their cumbersome ships back and forth as if they were on the bridges of destroyers.

The convoy commodore's ship, a brand new destroyer of the T class let a Heinkel have a full salvo with its 5-inch guns – to Andrews it seemed as if the ship leapt out of the water with the eruption of the main battery – and the plane disintegrated into nothing, save a lone wing which came fluttering like a falling leaf. A merchantman to her port got another and it sank quickly as it hit the sea. But still the Germans came on from all directions, dropping their two torpedoes and then heading east again, engines racing. The convoy took its first casualty. A munition ship was hit amidships, exploding with a tremendous roar. Tracer ammunition zig-zagging crazily into the grey sky. But when the thick white cloud of smoke cleared a little, the munition ship began to settle fast. Hastily the convoy commodore ordered one of the 'tail-end Charlies', Royal Navy trawlers, to stand by to pick up survivors. Andrews breathed a sigh of relief, and standing by his side, CPO Thirsk put his thoughts into words.

'Thank God, we don't have to tow that one back to port, sir!'

A Russian tanker was struck just forward of the engine room. Veering crazily, she broke out of her line. Andrews felt himself grip his binoculars fiercely as she just missed crashing into another ship. She began to belch thick black oily smoke. From her shattered side, oil spurted into the water. Still her gunners kept firing. Through his glasses, he could see that one of her machine guns was 'manned' by a fat dumpy woman in a bulky wadded jacket and, of all things, a skirt. He called Sparks.

'Get a message to the Convoy Commodore,' he rapped. 'Shall we stand by to help?'

'Ay, ay, sir!' The seaman doubled away to send the message by the R/T. Minutes later, he was back, panting hard. Cupping his hands around his mouth, he yelled above the roar and snarl of the Heinkels:

'No go sir! Convoy Commodore says carry on!' Andrews took a last look at the Russian tanker. It was falling behind rapidly, flames sweeping its deck. But the dumpy woman was still at the aft machine gun firing furiously at the Heinkels swooping up and down the convoy.

'All right, Sparks, carry on!' Andrews yelled.

Sparks hurried back towards his station. But in the confusion of the littered deck, with the *Rattlesnake*'s guns firing flat out, he caught one of his boots in the lanyard of a PAC rocket. As he sprawled flat on his face on the deck, the rocket went off, playing out its wire behind it, and crashed head-on into the last Heinkel directly overhead, still seeking a target for its two torpedoes. While Sparks lay gasping on the deck, his hands clasped over his ears against the tremendous noise above him, the wire sheered the plane's left wing neatly like a surgeon slicing off a useless limb. The plane dropped like a stone, while its wing floated gracefully behind it, crashed into the sea a hundred yards away and disappeared immediately, leaving the lone wing behind on the oil slick to prove that HMS *Rattlesnake* had made its first kill.

As the ratings scrambled to pick up a dazed Sparks, shouting at the top of their voices like crazy men, he realized that he was now a hero.

'Bloody hell,' he said in an awed voice, as they reached him and started to slap him joyously on the back, 'I've shot down a Jerry...'

They moved slowly through the oil-covered water, its waves subdued now by the spreading slick. To left and to right, there were crippled ships everywhere, but as far as Andrews could see they were still capable of moving under their own steam.

'Survivors, sir!' Erickson yelled. 'On the port!'

'Stand by to haul 'em up,' Andrews yelled, as the rope ladders started to go over the side.

There were about a dozen of them in the water, crying up weakly at the shock-faced ratings staring down at them, their faces black with oil. Erickson went over the side himself. As Andrews watched, the big ex-skipper hauled the first man out of the water with one hand.

'Get him below! Nelson's blood and blankets!' CPO Thirsk snapped. 'Come on now, look lively!'

Another man was hauled over the side,

shivering with cold, blood streaming across the black surface of his face from a deep gash in his head. He was followed by a small fat man who hadn't the strength to haul himself over. Hawkins, the strongest man in the ship after Erickson, reached out to take his hands. The fat survivor screamed and fell back into the water, leaving a horrified Hawkins staring down at the two fistfuls of burned flesh he had pulled off. As Erickson tried to fish the fat man out once again, Hawkins turned and began to be sick, his big shoulders heaving violently.

'Sir.'

A white-faced Andrews turned, glad for the break in the tension. It was Bunts.

'What is it?'

'Signal from the Convoy Commodore, sir.'

Behind him, CPO Thirsk was shouting to Erickson:

'Better leave him Charlie, he's had it... Get the bloke with the head wound.'

'We're to break off picking up survivors, sir. We're to leave it to that tail-end Charlie over there.' With a nod of his head, Bunts indicated the scruffy trawler hurrying towards them at top speed. 'The Convoy Commodore says we've got to have a look at the *American Hero* – that's her,' he indicated a large cargo ship to starboard which was firing distress rockets and was already beginning to lower its boats. 'Check whether we can tow.'

'All right, Bunts.' Andrews nodded. 'Signal Convoy Commodore will do.'

'Ay, ay, sir.' As Bunts sprang to the Aldis, Andrews bellowed across to CPO Thirsk:

'Break off the rescue operation, Chief. The trawler will pick 'em up!'

CPO Thirsk hesitated. He took a last look at the shocked, wounded men below in the sea. In their midst there was a dead man, an old seaman by the look of him, his grey head lolling from one side to another with the swell like that of a broken doll. No one would pick him up, and he would float like that for days until finally he sank into oblivion for good. Even those who had served with him in a succession of rusty old tubs, made love with him in cheap tropical brothels, drunk their pints with him in shabby dockside pubs would be dead too by now. Merchantseaman X, his cards stamped for good.

'All right, Charlie,' he called down to Erickson, 'Get up on deck. Skipper's orders. That trawler over there will pick up the rest. We've got a tow, I think.'

'The skipper's pissed as a newt,' the cock-eyed Hull man said irreverently as they strained up the steeply sloping deck of the *American Hero* towards the hatless captain.

'Hold your mouth,' snapped Andrews, as he fought his way through the smashed debris. 'Even if he is, he deserves it after this!' He gestured towards the confused mess of torn rail and bridge house.

'Hi there feller,' the American captain said, clutching the half empty bottle of bourbon in his right hand, as if his life depended upon it, 'welcome aboard.' He took a quick swig of the drink, belched and wiped the back of his hand across his lips with a suddenly satisfied smile. 'What can I do for you?'

'Lieutenant Andrews HMS *Rattlesnake,* sir. The convoy commodore asked me to check whether you are capable of being towed.'

The American tugged the end of his bulbous nose, the result of too much drink and exposure to Arctic winds, and shook his head.

'Negative. The old *American Zero – Zero,* you get it? – is about to cash in her chips, young feller.'

'Do you mind if I have a look, sir?'

Andrews asked politely.

'Not at all.' He threw out his big hand in an expansive gesture and nearly overbalanced on the steep deck. 'Be my guest.'

'Chief, you keep an eye on the situation up here, I'll go down with the master,' Andrews ordered. 'Check that the crew is standing by.'

'Ay, ay, sir,' snapped CPO Thirsk, eyeing the drunken American captain in his stained wrinkled uniform with undisguised disgust. 'All right, you men, work your way across the deck and do as the Captain sez!'

Together with the American skipper, Andrews fought his way across the grievously stricken vessel, their progress accompanied by the older man's heavy breathing and the regular belches of the giant air bubbles gouting from the ship's holed side. The galley door hung open. Andrews peered inside and wished next moment he hadn't. Floating in the confused mess of potatoes, tins, loaves of bread, suspended by his rubber lifebelt, the cook bellied back and forth, fully dressed, his body without a blemish, save that it was minus a head. The American skipper laughed at the Navy man's horrified expression.

'Couldn't have happened to a nicer guy,' he chuckled and took another swig of the bourbon. 'That goddam cook could even burn shit on shingle.' He meant mincemeat on toast.

They struggled on, fighting their way through the mangled mess of metal, contorted into fantastic, obscene shapes by the force of the two torpedoes which had struck the *American Hero.* What was left of the main smoke stack hung at a giddy angle, supported by a mere fragment of metal. Most of the bridge and the captain's cabin had gone too. But the port bridge wing was still intact, but somehow the Oerlikon had been twisted completely round by the blast and now the dead gunner hung in the harness, his long blond hair dangling in the water like a fern.

'My son Joe's boy,' the Merchant skipper said matter-of-factly. 'All of eighteen, dropped out of his freshman year at college to come with me.' He shrugged and took another drink of the fiery spirit. 'What could I do? First trip too. God knows what Joe'll say. But he was at Pearl on the Seventh.' He chuckled absurdly. 'Perhaps he got the chop too, eh!'

Lieutenant Andrews did not know how to answer. Nothing in his previous twenty-two years had prepared him for so much violent death and the calm way that the others – Erickson, Thirsk, this American Captain – seemed to accept it as a normal condition of life. Suddenly he wished he were back in Eastbourne, hiding from all this horror in the familiar surroundings of one of his mother's genteel afternoon teas with the old ladies and the polite chit-chat that had nothing to do with the real world. But he knew that he was responsible for the fates of twenty-eight other men and indirectly for the fate of all those connected with them.

'Could I just have a peek at the rest, sir?'

'Sure, have a peek!' the American sneered. 'Peek as much as you goddam like!'

Five minutes later Andrews knew that the *American Hero* would not stand up to the long tow to Murmansk. She was too badly holed and the water was rushing in below decks at a tremendous rate. He stopped his tour in the officers' wardroom. Half-filled bottles of coke were still standing on one of the tables – in spite of the captain's bourbon, the ship was officially 'dry' – and on the settee in the corner, the ship's cat lay curled up on a cushion as if it were asleep, but the cushion was soaked with blood. The American skipper stroked it idly, then recoiled when he realized the animal was dead.

'Poor little bastard,' he said, and took a quick swig of the bottle. 'Best rat catcher I've ever known in forty years at sea.' His voice rose. 'Okay, son, what's the deal. Do you tow?'

''Fraid not, sir. You're too badly holed. We'd never make it.'

'I see.' He offered Andrews the bottle. 'Like a shot?'

'No thank you, sir. I don't really drink.' Andrews flushed.

'You will, you will son, before you've finished with this war... Okay, so you're gonna ditch the old *American Zero*.' He drained what was left of the bottle and tossed it away carelessly. 'Give me five to get a couple of things together, will ya?'

'Certainly, sir. But please hurry – we're in danger from further attacks.'

The Captain looked at him strangely.

'Sure, I'll make it snappy, son. And – listen – thanks.'

He staggered off towards what was left of his cabin, while Andrews struggled his way back on to the main deck where CPO Thirsk was waiting for him anxiously.

'Better get our fingers out, sir,' he said. 'I don't think she's going to last much longer.'

'Yes Chief, I'm just waiting for the skipper

to get his gear together. Then we'll abandon her. Everybody cleared?'

'Yes sir. I've got them rowing over to one of those tail-end Charlies. They can look–'

The rest of his words were drowned by the single revolver shot. When they got to the captain's cabin, already half-awash with sea-water, he was dead, the big revolver dropping slowly from his lifeless fingers.

'Pissed as a newt,' was the cock-eyed Hull man's comment. 'I told you he was…'

'Scouse and sodding spotty Dick!' Bunts cursed bitterly, looking down at the Christmas dinner spread out on the heaving mess-table. 'You know what yer can do with yer sodding Christmas pudden, sarnt-major!'

'Are you speaking to me, Bunts?' CPO Thirsk snapped, as he helped Erickson to dish out the poor fare, making an attempt to keep up the Royal Navy tradition of the petty officers serving the men at Christmas.

'No, Chief,' Bunts said. 'But it's funny kind of grub to serve up to a bloke on Christmas Day. You'd think that sodding cook could have done a bit better than this.'

'We're on hard tack and bully tomorrow, mate,' Sparks chimed in happily. 'That last attack put the galley fire out and the cook can't get it started again.'

'You're a right ray of sunshine, you are,' his mate Bunts grunted and set about the food which was already beginning to congeal with the cold.

Thirsk looked at them. They were very tired, their eyes bloodshot, their faces haggard, most of them were distinctly dirty and unshaven. In the ablutions the flannels were as hard as board and the soap frozen to the washbowls. Not that many of them liked more than a cat's lick at the best of times, he told himself, and now they had a good excuse for not indulging in any excessive personal cleanliness. By the time they got to Murmansk, most of them would be stinking to high heaven.

'Charlie,' he said to Erickson, who had finished handing out the mess tins of spotty Dick pudding, 'see if you can get a bit of music on the radio to cheer this lot of happy heroes up, will you?'

Erickson twirled the knobs of the ancient radio, which the crew had pooled together in a Hull pub to buy from a docker who said he had found it in James Street after a raid. Suddenly a harsh, well-known voice cut into the celebration.

'And one wonders, ladies and gentlemen,'

it said with its familiar nasal insinuation, 'how the sailormen of convoy PQ 8 will be spending the festive season? My friends of the German Kreigsmarine tell me they are prepared to make it a warm, if wet one for them at least. Like they did for the other two and a half million tons of British shipping which Admiral Doenitz's brave submariners have sunk since June–'

'Turn that sod off, Erickson!' Thirsk snapped angrily. Swiftly Erickson swung the dial round until the cheerful booming voice of Mrs Mopp filled the suddenly silent room with her standard question of whether she could 'do you now sir?' But the damage had been done, and it could not be dispelled by the quickfire repartee of Tommy Handley and the rest of the ITMA cast.

'The buggers know we're coming,' a gloomy Bunts summed it up for them. 'That sod Lord Haw-Haw knows what he's talking about. When Hull got its first big bashing last year, he even gave the time the town hall clock had stopped at. He's got his spies everywhere.'

'Go on,' Hawkins, the Londoner, countered. 'How the hell can he know? The Jerries have just got our convoy number that's all, and that don't mean much.'

But the English traitor's words hit home and in a way Thirsk was glad when the alarm gong started to sound again and they had to abandon what was left of the scouse and spotty Dick to man their battle stations yet once again, leaving the 'Mayor of Foaming-at-the-Mouth' to chatter on to himself.

The Junkers came in at sea-level – fifty of them, broken up into three large groups coming in from port and starboard. This time the Germans were making no attempt at evasion. They were coming in for the kill, relying on their superior speed and overwhelming numbers to swamp the convoy's defences.

The pilots were supremely confident, their nerves jingling with preludin, their ears still full of their commanders' promises: the Knight's Cross for every escort sunk, the German Cross in Gold for every merchantman, and the Iron Cross for every crew member if anything was sunk, plus ten days' leave in the Homeland. Boldly they swept into battle, taking suicidal risks. The first plane received a direct hit from one of the destroyers and disappeared. A moment later another followed. A third, its wings shot off, dived straight into the sea like a wild duck.

But still they came on.

The barrage mounted in intensity. Every weapon available was being employed, regardless of the ammunition situation, for the gunners had grasped instinctively that this was the Luftwaffe's major and final attack. Even the merchantmen's Holman Projector, the joke of the whole fleet was employed, firing hand grenades into the sky by means of steam from the engine room. For the last two days, the Holmans had been used by joking merchant navy men to fire hot potatoes at one another across the water; now the 'hot potato cart', as they had nicknamed it, was being used in deadly earnest.

The leader of the port group was hit. It faltered in mid-air, plunged on to the nearest merchantman and skidded along its deck, taking bridge and superstructure with it in a searing burst of flame. When the flame cleared, the plane had gone and the merchantman's deck was a shattered wreck.

'Christ almighty!' Bunts breathed, standing by at Andrews' side, 'Did you see that, sir? That Jerry deliberately took a nose-dive on the merchantman!'

But Andrews had no time for the merchantman; the Germans were coming in relentlessly, pressing home their attack with fanatical energy despite their casualties. Another Junkers blew up in mid-air and he saw the pilot come sailing out, head tucked in, hands clasped around his knees in the foetal position, bowling through the convoy, like a human cricket ball. One of the escorts was hit. Through his binoculars Andrews could see the safety valves bursting and spouting billowing clouds of white smoke. Even at that distance, he could smell the acrid and nauseous odour of the burning ship.

'Take a signal, Bunts,' he yelled above the ear-splitting din of the *Rattlesnake*'s Oerlikons. 'Do you need help?'

Moments later the frigate's answer came blinking back:

'In the words of Eliza Doolittle – not bloody likely. This is the Royal Navy, not the Wavy one!'

A puzzled Bunts looked at Andrews as he read it.

'What's it mean, sir – Eliza Doolittle?'

'Oh nothing, Bunts,' Andrews answered, grinning despite himself. Even the reference to the fact that HMS *Rattlesnake* was commanded by a reserve officer in the 'wavy navy' – did not sour the brave humour of the stricken ship's message.

The battle went on. A tanker was hit and the entire front of the ship folded up like an enormous banana skin. There was no hope of saving her; the flames were already beginning to lick up greedily from her hull. Even before Andrews could signal, a destroyer was there ready to torpedo the tanker as soon as the survivors were evacuated by one of the tail-end Charlies. And now the Commander of the Fifth Air Field in Norway was sending in that weapon which had been so successful on every battlefield in Western Europe in these last two years – the Stuka.

They came roaring in after the departing Junkers, two squadrons of them, flying in perfect formation, for their pilots were Goering's elite, pre-war trained, their blue-grey uniformed chests stiff with the decorations gained in Spain, Poland, France, Greece and Russia.

'Here they come!' Erickson bellowed, as the Stuka leader up-ended suddenly like a swimmer diving off a board. 'Stand by yer guns!'

The crews needed no urging. As the first flight peeled off, they commenced a furious barrage, which was taken up all along the battered convoy. The first shape threw itself out of the evening sky, its twin sirens screaming hideously. Black puffballs of ack-ack burst all around it. Red and white tracer converged on it in a deadly, visible morse. Just when it seemed that the plane must plunge nose-first into the sea, the pilot pulled it out of its tremendous dive. A myriad black eggs cascaded from the white-painted belly, churning the sea around one of the escorts into a series of enormous waterspouts. To a horrified Andrews, it seemed that no ship could survive in that maelstrom. But when the water subsided, it revealed the destroyer rolling violently from side to side, but still undamaged.

One after another the Stukas hurtled out of the sky blinding the convoy with the smoke of their bombs, the noise of their engines deafening as they screamed in again and again for the kill. Here and there a Stuka was struck, shattering in mid-air, snuffed out suddenly like a candle, or plunging into the sea at 400 mph. But still the survivors came on, standing in line out of range of the convoy's guns, preparing to make their dive attack and then swooping in on the ships below.

On the HMS *Rattlesnake,* the gunners

began to flag, all except Erickson who seemed tireless. CPO Thirsk ordered up the off-duty watch to take over, and seizing the twin machine guns himself despite the pain of his rheumaticky knees, poured a vicious stream of white and red lead at a Stuka. The terrible howl grew louder.

'Don't fire so bloody low!' Thirsk cried at another gunner, 'You're hitting the next ruddy ship!' A loud squeal like that of a trapped and dying animal. A stick of bombs plunging towards them.

'Hit the deck!' yelled Erickson urgently.

On the bridge, Andrews had a momentary glimpse of a blinding white light, ringed in violet. Then the deck came up to meet him. As the *Rattlesnake* shuddered crazily, the blast hit the rim of his helmet and knocked it backwards off his head. He felt an excruciating pain in his ears.

'Don't let go,' an inner voice commanded. 'For Christ sake, *don't let go!'*

As he fell to his knees on the wet deck, littered with debris of the raid he felt the darkness closing in on him.

When he came to, the raid was over and the Stukas – what were left of them – were winging rapidly away back to Norway. No one had seen him black out, for which he was thankful. He pulled himself to his feet. The helmsman had been too busy steering the ship in a crazy zig-zag through the bombs to have noticed his predicament.

'Carry, on, helmsman,' he said in voice that seemed very far away. He swallowed hard and the steady beat-beat of the *Rattlesnake*'s engines came back at their normal level. 'I'm going to have a look-see at the damage.'

'Ay, ay, sir,' the deathly-pale rating replied, his eyes fixed on the water, full of wreckage and bodies, dead and alive.

Brushing the damp mess off his knees, Andrews clattered down the iron ladder. The deck was littered with fist-sized pieces of shrapnel and gleaming brass shell-cases thrown down from the gun platforms. One of the lifeboats was hanging at an angle, its woodwork ripped to pieces by machine-gun fire, with an arm hanging limply over one side. Andrews ran towards the arm and tugged – its owner had to be rescued before the remaining ropes gave way and the shattered boat fell into the sea. But the arm came away in his hand, and he nearly overbalanced. Retching violently, he flung it down.

'Captain!'

It was Thirsk, his cap gone, his leathery face streaked with black powder burns, his hands red with blood to the wrists.

'They're down here.'

'Who?' he quavered.

'Our two lads who got hit – and the Jerry. That last stick was a close bastard. The shrapnel got Pontey' – he meant the cock-eyed Hull man – 'and Beaconsfield, the cook's mate.'

'And the Jerry?'

'Just dropped out of the clouds, sir. As naked as the day as he was born except that – well, you'd better come and have a look, sir.'

Reluctantly Andrews followed the stiff-legged CPO down the steep ladder into the dark, cramped crews' quarters, his nose already assailed by a ghastly stench. The oil-soaked survivors were squatting on the wet floor between the bunks, drinking rum, shivering with cold and fear, and then retching into the zinc bowls which someone had placed in front of them. Next to them the two wounded men lay stretched out. The cook's ear had been severed and he was holding it while Erickson tried to sew it on again with a thick curved needle, cursing monotonously as the blood soaked his fingers and the stitches he had already made. Beside them a cold pool of blood was forming on the floor as it trickled from the still figure of the cock-eyed man from Hull.

'Oh my God,' Andrews exclaimed, and swayed.

Thirsk grabbed his arm and forced his big fingers into Andrews' bicep.

'Steady on, sir,' he hissed. 'Don't let the crew see you!'

'But that man–'

'He's had it, sir,' Thirsk hissed again, his voice harsh and urgent. 'His left arm was sheered off. Nothing we can do. Erickson pumped him full of dope to kill him off. At least he can kick off without too much pain. But the Jerry,' he shook his grey head, 'God knows what we can do for that poor bastard – he's still conscious.'

'Where is he?' Andrews asked, forcing himself to keep his voice steady.

'I put him in the latrines.'

'In the latrines!' Andrews recoiled.

'Wait till you see him, sir,' Thirsk said grimly.

The Stuka pilot sat upright, his back propped against one of the latrines, his arms outstretched with the hands propped up on two zinc buckets. From the feet upwards, he was a normal man, feet still clad in fur-lined flying boots, strong, powerfully-muscled legs. But from the waist up the German had sustained deep burns. From waist to throat the surface of his upper body looked as if it had been flayed with a whip and then roasted on a kitchen spit.

'This is the poor bastard,' Thirsk said softly.

Andrews forced himself to bend down and look at the man's horrible red skull of a face, bereft of hair, eyebrows and ears. Perhaps it might have been the soft touch of his breath on the German's naked flesh, but whatever it was, he opened his eyes at once and a whimper of pain escaped from the lipless mouth.

'How is it, old man?' Andrews asked, knowing if he didn't say something he would scream aloud with the horror of it all.

'Mensch,' the German groaned, *'lass mich doh krepieren!'*

Andrews looked at the CPO helplessly.

'What did he say, Chief?'

Thirsk shrugged.

'Search me, sir. I don't understand German.'

Andrews gritted his teeth.

'Chief, what have we got for him? Surely

we've got something to ease the pain?'

'Aspros, sir. I've got a dozen Aspros. I take 'em for me knees, sir.'

'Stop that, Chief,' Andrews snapped. 'This man's a human being, even if he is a Jerry! We've got to help him. I don't like that kind of joke.'

'It's not a joke. That's all we've got, sir. Erickson's used all the morphia on the other bloke.'

'Oh my Christ. Well, we've got something for the burns surely? We can't let him suffer like this. The fellow's in terrible pain.'

'There's flour in the galley.'

'You can't use flour,' Andrews retorted. 'Any schoolkid knows that's no use for burns.'

CPO Thirsk took his gaze off the German and looked at Andrews, his tired eyes full of tears.

'I know that, sir. But that's all we've got and a tin of brassic ointment.'

'Gib mir dock eine Pistole,' the German croaked suddenly. *'Lass mich doch Schluss machen!'*

'What did he say?' Thirsk asked.

Behind him Erickson rose to his feet stiffly.

'Four-eyes has had it,' he announced,

bloody curved needle still clasped in his hand. 'Somebody cover him up with a blanket.'

'I thought he said something about pistol,' Andrews answered.

'*Ja Pistole*,' the German said, his eyes scanning their faces eagerly. He attempted to make the gesture of pulling a trigger with his forefinger and whimpered with pain as the taut pink flesh split open.

'Get me some oil,' Andrews said, 'some of that olive oil that the cook uses.'

'Ay, ay, sir.' It was Sparks who had approached on tip-toe, scared that slightest movement might give pain to the German sprawled out in the wet stinking latrine among the scraps of paper torn from old newspapers. He doubled away quickly.

But it was no use. As he tried to dab it on him, the German screamed out loud. Andrews persisted grimly, the sweat trickling down his face with tension. But the cotton wool stuck to the man's tortured flesh and once when his hand slipped the swab tore away a long strip of the red surface to reveal the gleaming whiteness of a rib beneath. Twice the German fainted and when he came to, he pleaded for *die Pistole* with a look of animal despair in his eyes. Sparks, standing above him, turned his head away and snarled.

'For fuck's sake, man, why don't you sodding well die!'

But the injured Stuka pilot simply refused to die. He lingered on interminably, his breath becoming more shallow, pleading at regular intervals for a pistol to shoot himself. It was only when they heard the hollow echoing boom of a ship being struck, and the *Rattlesnake* shuddered violently, indicating that the enemy was attacking again, that he slumped dead to the wet bloody mess of the latrine floor.

'Bugger it,' Erickson yelled, as Andrews and the CPO came running on the bridge, 'now it's the sodding U-boats!'

'Where?' Andrews cried, grabbing his binoculars.

'Starboard, sir. Right up at the top of the third lane. That big grain ship, sir! She's going down fast.'

As the escorts swung into their anti-sub attack formation, their sirens screaming, Andrews frantically focused his glasses. Against the blood-red of the setting sun, a half-circle on the horizon, he fixed on the grain ship. She had been struck amidships and was sinking fast. Tiny black figures, starkly silhouetted against the sun, were throwing themselves over the side. Lifeboats were being lowered in panicky haste. On her steeply sloping deck men were running to and fro like ants.

'Are you sure it's a sub, Erickson?' Andrews asked quickly, lowering his glasses.

'Certain, sir. No mines this far north. Besides I've heard enough of the bastards to know the difference between a mine and a torpedo.'

'Okay, stand by then for orders from the Convoy Commodore–' He broke off. A set of flags was running up the Convoy Commodore's flag hoist. 'Bunts, what's that say?'

Bunts strained his eyes against the setting sun. He shook his head. An anxious Andrews could see his lips forming the words.

'Well?' he cried.

'I don't rightly know whether I've read it proper, sir,' Bunts said lamely.

'For God's sake, what did it say, man?' Andrews exploded.

'Well, I think it says – all convoy scatter. Subs. Proceed Russian ports–' He broke off suddenly. 'Here, wait a mo, sir, it's coming over the lamp now. *All convoy scatter and proceed to Russian ports. Escorts – negative destroyers – proceed independently to Archangel.*'

He broke off and then after a moment uttered what they were all thinking.

'Bloody hellus, sir! This is where the sodding fun and games start!'

He was right. As the sun finally slid over the horizon, covering the scattering of the convoy in blessed darkness, the U-boats came in for the kill, knowing now that they would be in no danger from the escorts. On the flag hoist of the convoy commodore, the signal Charlie-Mike went up and the light escorts swung into formation to obey the order 'join me' in the prescribed defence pattern.

And then the wolf pack was among the terrified merchantmen. The night was ripped apart by the explosions of their torpedoes as yet another merchantman keeled over and sunk. Within five minutes of the message from the convoy commodore the survivors were zig-zagging in every direction in their panic-stricken flight from the German attack.

At exactly ten minutes after eight, the SS *St George* was hit, illuminated momentarily by a brilliant flash of white flame as the torpedo struck her. On the horizon the convoy commodore's aldis flicked off and on in urgent summons to the *Rattlesnake* to investigate the situation.

'Sorry to leave you like this, Wavy Navy,' the hurried message concluded. *'Looks like being a bloody business. Goodbye and good luck.'*

Then the aldis died and HMS *Rattlesnake* was alone on the dark rolling ocean with nothing in sight save the dull, steady flicker of the burning *St George* on the horizon.

DAY FIVE: DECEMBER 26th, 1941

'We like your looks, Wavy Navy. We think you'll get us through!'

Captain, SS St George to
Lieutenant Andrews.

'Object ahead, sir!' the wizened little Petty Officer rapped, lowering his night glasses and turning to Hartmann, his oilskin slick with the spray thrown up by the bow.

'Where?'

'Green one-zero, sir!' the Obermaat yelled.

Hartmann levelled his binoculars in the direction indicated by the Obermaat. For a moment he could see nothing. Then he felt a wave of fierce excitement pass over him. As the U-122 dipped abruptly, he caught a glimpse of superstructure and funnels on the horizon, stark black against the solid grey of the Arctic sky. It vanished almost instantaneously, but Hartmann had not spent many long hours poring over the recognition charts for nothing.

'Enemy merchantman,' he announced to the conning-tower, fighting back his excitement. 'Eighteen thousand tonner. Green-zero-one!'

There was a gasp of surprise from the watch.

'Great crap on the Christmas tree!' Dietz exclaimed, 'the Tommies are here already.'

'So it would seem,' he answered coldly, although the blood was pulsing furiously through his veins. He raised his voice above the howl of the Arctic wind. 'All right, everyone, action stations!'

Fifteen minutes later U-122 was steady, an invisible killer, hidden deep in the waves, its grey silhouette indistinguishable against the black mass of Bear Island behind it. Tensely the crew waited at their posts, their faces almost luminous in the yellow light, beads of sweat forming in the roots of their hair. On the bridge, Hartmann, his night glasses glued to his eyes, the muscles of his face under the blond beard set and hard, watched the unsuspecting Tommy ship looming closer. Obviously the enemy captain was relying on the ship's superior speed to get him through to Murmansk without an escort. Hartmann smiled coldly to himself: the Tommy Captain was in for a big surprise.

'Tubes one to four – ready for surface fire, sir!' the forrard torpedo petty officer reported, startling him out of his reverie.

'Tubes one to four – ready for surface fire!' the aft NCO repeated.

Down below the torpedo officer was over his instruments, adjusting his killer weapons to every delicate nuance indicated by the petty officer crouched at the range-finder, his face strained and tense in the dim-white light.

'Target Green 90, speed fifteen knots, range six thousand metres!' the man at the range-finder called out.

Hartmann ran through the same rapid calculation that the torpedo officer was making at that moment below in the tight stinking confines of the U-boat. Target speed fifteen knots, torpedo speed 30 knots, angle of torpedo approach to target 90°, crossing the U-122's bows from right to left. That meant he would have to lay off at an angle of 45° on the periscope and that the centre torpedo of the salvo would have to be fired when the target was 45° on their starboard bow. Thus he would be looking north east through the periscope at the same time as he was firing a torpedo steering north. It was a tricky procedure but all the U-122's officers had gone through the attack teacher's 'box', the dummy periscope, at Müwik and should be able to carry out the complicated procedure in their sleep. All the same, with such a tempting target sailing so boldly in front of his eyes, Hartmann was taking no chances: after all the lump of metal six kilometres away meant the award of the precious piece of tin for him.

'Lined up, sir,' the torpedo officer reported suddenly from below.

He had connected the attack table with the gyro-compass and attack sight. Beyond the attack table the twin red lights indicated that the information being fed in had not been completed. Meanwhile firing settings were being transmitted automatically to the torpedoes and set on their angling mechanism.

Hartmann, crouched on the bridge, fighting the flying spray which threatened to blind him every other moment, could see the enemy ship quite clearly now: a modern merchantman, laid down in some northern English yard before the war in the bad years as a symbol of British hope in the future.

'Ready?' he snapped to the torpedo officer.

'Ready!' he answered. 'Ready, captain.'

'Thank you. Fire at four thousand five

hundred metres. Aim at the foremast… Rate of turn, green three.'

With mounting tension, Hartmann heard the East Frisian Lüttjens call the torpedo petty officer.

'Green three. Stand by for surface fire.'

Without turning, Hartmann called to the helmsman:

'Hard-a-starboard.' The torpedo petty officers carried the litany a stage further:

'Bow tubes – stand by for surface fire!'

'Tubes one, three and four ready, sir!'

Hartmann took one last look at the unsuspecting British ship; then, heart thumping wildly beneath the soaked oilskins, he said:

'Fire when ready.'

Lüttjens could not conceal his excitement.

'Fertig!' he cried, his voice almost breaking.

'On … on …on!' the torpedo petty officers called back.

Below, Lüttjens, tensely keeping the enemy ship's foremast in the crosswires of the periscope, yelled:

'Feuer!'

'Feuer!' the petty officers echoed.

Below, the torpedo officer pulled out his watch hastily and checked the seconds off as the first torpedo hissed towards its unsuspecting target. But Hartmann had no eyes for his watch. Feeling a sense of almost sexual relief as the boat shuddered every one and one-fifth seconds to each new torpedo, he flung up his glasses to observe the merchantman.

The engineers below were already flooding the tanks to compensate for the loss of the torpedoes' weight, ready for an instant crash-dive. Behind him the petty officer at the range finder was counting off the seconds. Hartmann gripped his binoculars savagely, as the merchantman sailed on calmly, unaware of its impending fate. The sweat trickled down his forehead in spite of the cold.

'We've *got* to hit her,' he whispered to himself. 'We've got to!'

Suddenly he heard the unmistakable sound of a torpedo striking home. For a moment the British ship sailed on, as if nothing had happened. Then her bow rose steeply into the grey dawn sky – Hartmann could see the red paint below the waterline quite distinctly. From below there came the first muffled cheer.

'We've hit her, sir!' the officer-cadet standing behind him cried exultantly. 'We've sunk the Tommy! Look – she's beginning to fall apart!'

He was right. Great chunks of metal began to fly into the sky, as the explosives the merchantman contained caught fire.

'Yes, it does look like it,' Hartmann said drily, while his mind raced crazily, imagining the presentation of the Knight's Cross at the *Berghof*, the reception at his Father's divisional HQ when he was flown in to see him by special permission of the Greater German General Staff, the 'Big Lion' shaking him by the hand and granting him two weeks' special leave, the look on the girls' faces in Hamburg's *Alsterpavillion* as he strolled in with the coveted decoration carelessly dangling around his neck.

'Sir.' Dietz broke into his reverie as the British ship began to sink rapidly on the horizon.

'Yes, what is it?'

'The Tommy is sending out an SOS and our position – and that's not all, sir. A Tommy destroyer has answered – and it's just over the horizon, sir!'

'Ping ... ping ... ping!' the tinny, ominous sound of the destroyer's range finder came closer and closer. In the hot, stinking interior of the U-122 everyone was sweating, but not with the heat.

'It's not just anybody who gets such an expensive coffin,' Berlin Big Mouth remarked drily. 'Four million marks to be put away like this.'

'Halt deint Berliner Schnause!' the wizened Obermaat cried. 'Berliners – always running off at the trap. One of these shitty days, somebody's gonna stop it–'

'Be quiet!' Hartmann ordered. 'No talking. Our oxygen is short enough as it is.'

Hartmann fell silent again, but he could understand the crew; their inability to defend themselves against the destroyer was maddening and this trapped inactivity almost unbearable. But the alternative was worse: surface and fight it out with the much superior Tommy destroyer. Hartmann looked at his watch. Forty-five minutes had passed since they had dived. The fun would start soon.

'All right,' he said quietly, looking around at their tense faces, 'stand by to receive depth-charges. From now – silent routine.'

Hartmann felt a cold bead of sweat trickle slowly down the small of his back. Across from him the officer-cadet was playing with his fingers. Dietz, who had been through this before, was taking deep, slow breaths, his mouth slightly open, so that the first explosion would not burst his eardrums. Only Frisian Lüttjens seemed unaffected, but then, Hartmann told himself contemptuously, the East Frisians were famous for their thick-headed stupidity.

Suddenly there was a sharp metallic click. He tensed. He had heard that terrible sound twice before. It was the firing mechanism of a depth charge, preceding the explosion by half a second. The next instant an inferno of ear-splitting, bone-shaking chaos was loosed upon them. They were flung from side to side as the gush of water – tons of it – hit the U-122. In the lunatic confusion of crashing glass and cursing men, with the lights flickering off and on insanely, the U-boat crew swept to the floor.

Hartmann clung desperately to the control-room ladder, ducking his head as light bulbs shattered everywhere and fractured glass hissed through the interior. The U-122 shook violently. As more and more explosions followed, he had that swimming, detached feeling he had once experienced as a cadet in the old sailing ship when another cadet had given him a stiff right to the jaw.

'Stand fast!' he yelled frantically as the lights went out suddenly. *'Stand fast, men!'*

Dietz reacted first. He switched on the little torch clipped to his salt-stained tunic and rising to his feet, pulled the emergency light switch. The boat flooded with a weak yellow light again. Hartmann flung a glance at the barometer glass. It looked all right. He rapped it with his knuckles. The green-painted needle moved. A slight increase in pressure – no more. If the U-122 had been holed by the first depth charge attack, the damage couldn't be so serious. He swallowed hard.

'Report your damage,' he ordered softly.

One by one the subdued replies came back. *'Ales in Ordnung … nichts zu melden … klar Schiff…'*

Hartmann breathed a sigh of relief. *'Danke mein Herren,'* he replied and blinked rapidly. His eyes were beginning to itch now.

Above them the propellers were racing again as the Tommy destroyer came in for another attack. Hartmann held on to the ladder tightly once more. He knew instinctively it was too early to attempt to take any form of evasive drill. The Tommy skipper wouldn't buy the odd pair of boots and a few old clothes fired out of the torpedo tube as evidence that he had sunk the German submarine – and they didn't have a dead man – as yet – to convince him. They would have to endure another attack before he could try that particular trick on the English.

'Sir,' it was the officer-cadet. 'Sir, *the batteries!'*

Now Hartmann understood why his throat was beginning to hurt and why the emergency lighting was growing steadily dimmer. The electric batteries had been hit and were flooding the U-122 with acrid gas which resulted from their coming into contact with seawater.

The noise of the British destroyer was getting louder and louder. Hartmann licked his lips and looked up at the dim lights desperately. Next to him, the wizened old PO from Hamburg scribbled something on a piece of paper with a stub of pencil and handed it to him. Hartmann pushed it away, but the old man persisted. Straining his eyes, he read it:

'Maydag, Hannes, Obermaat. Requests permission to go back to General Service Duties immediately.'

Hartmann laughed out loud and handed the message over to Dietz. Slowly it went from one grinning rating to the next as the roar of the Tommy's propellers seemed to shake their very bones. But even as he laughed, Hartmann knew that if the Tommy did not get them, the creeping gas would.

'Ahoy there,' Andrews called through the loud-hailer, staring up at the stricken tanker which loomed up above them. Next to him an anxious CPO Thirsk searched the crumpled upper deck, still glowing with the heat of the swiftly extinguished fire; and Andrews knew why. He was looking for his son. But in the darkness the figures far above remained anonymous voices.

'Ahoy, there, HMS *Rattlesnake!'* a thick voice, full of beer and years of command, called back. 'Is that the captain?'

'Yes sir.' Andrews did not wait for a reply. He was a sitting duck as it was; he didn't want to make it too easy for the Jerry sub captains.

'What's the situation, can we tow, captain?'

'We've been hit in the engine room – and they're out. The stern's badly flooded, but she's buoyant all right. I reckon we're drawing about twenty foot of water.'

'Bloody hell, did you hear that,' Bunts exploded to Erickson and Sparks, while

Andrews considered the information from the tanker captain. 'What's yon Mary Ann with his la-di-da accent think he's on! If we tow that sod, it'll be like pulling a bomb behind us!'

Erickson rounded on him angrily.

'Shut your filthy mouth, Bunts, or I'll shut it for you!'

'What did I say, Sparks?' Bunts asked the radio man in genuine bewilderment.

'I'll tell you, you git! That tanker isn't just a bit of floating metal, Bunts. There are men on board here – lads from the East Coast like us. From Withernsea, Brid, Hull, Goole, Scarboro. They're our mates, Bunts!'

Bunts was unimpressed.

'They're no mates o'mine,' he said grumpily, and lapsed into disgruntled silence.

Andrews had made up his mind.

'All right, captain, shall we give it a try?' he called up at the dark shape on the tanker through the loud-hailer. 'Would you stand by for a line?'

Before Andrews could pick up the rocket pistol himself, Thirsk stepped forward.

'Do you mind if I do it, sir?' he asked.

Andrews understood immediately.

'Of course, Chief, your son. Right, make it snappy.'

Trying to forget the aching pain in his knees, CPO Thirsk strode to the heaving bow and balanced himself against the roll, sizing up the distance between himself and the stricken *St George*. Watching him, Erickson could guess what was going through the old Chief's head: was his boy among the casualties in the shattered engine room? But he knew that Thirsk would never ask the skipper to find out from the tanker's captain. Thirsk and his kind kept their thoughts to themselves. As Erickson spat into the heaving water and hoped that Thirsk would be accurate, he knew he would never be like the CPO; his kind had had it. They were manning a sinking ship. They were the past and Erickson knew that the future belonged to arseholes like Bunts. But he, Erickson, didn't want to belong to that kind of future.

Thirsk bit his lip and aimed up at the *St George*'s lee. Normally he would have avoided the position because a big ship with more surface to the wind would drift off faster than a smaller one and there was always the danger that it could overrun any vessel to leeward of her. But there was no time now, with Jerry subs hovering around, for fancy security measures. He had to act quick. He pressed the trigger. The pistol jerked in his big gnarled hand. A spurt of flame, followed by a trail of fiery sparks, and the line snaked out and up. Thirsk bit back a curse. The wind caught the line and blew it almost parallel to the *St George*.

'Come on you bastard!' he cried to himself as the wind threatened to drive it away from the tanker at any moment. 'Hit the sod!'

Just as it seemed as if the wind would drag the grapnel completely off course, the projectile snagged in a piece of broken rigging hanging over the tanker's side. A dozen eager hands grabbed at it before it could fall to the sea below. Immediately the men of the tanker began to pull in the messenger line, while on the bridge Erickson and the Captain kept the little tug from being overrun by the massive bulk of the tanker until the line was firmly secured.

Andrews rapped out his orders swiftly. HMS *Rattlesnake* forged ahead and took the strain. Struggling desperately the ship fought the sea. And the sea fought back. The wind howled angrily, flinging spume and water smoke as high as her masthead as the *Rattlesnake* churned crazily to bring the stricken ship round. But it seemed as the sea were winning. Slowly but definitely, the tug and tow were being blown east.

On the heaving bridge, Erickson, Thirsk and Andrews fought back against the howl of the wind and the strained creak of the *Rattlesnake*'s metal. Erickson, sweat pouring down his body, feet braced, battled with the wheel, while Andrews cursed and yelled at the engine room, which couldn't give him the power he needed to turn the huge hulk of a tanker into the wind. Thirsk, for his part, doubled back and forth, checking the tow, urging the crew on to greater efforts, reassuring the tanker's captain through the loud-hailer. And then, suddenly, the sea gave in. The fierce wind dropped. The water-smoke washing over their bows subsided and all at once the great tanker was coming round into the wind. From across the narrow gap which separated them, the panting, sweating men on the bridge caught the snatch of a faint cheer. Erickson relaxed on the wheel for a moment and held up a thumb of triumph. Thirsk's leathery face cracked into a wary smile.

'We done it, skipper!'

Lieutenant Andrews felt like taking off his salt-stained cap and flinging it into the air with elation, but he knew that even a Wavy Navy officer could not afford the luxury of such an emotion. He contented himself, therefore, with a polite, restrained Eastbourne:

'It rather looks like it, doesn't it?'

Despite his elation, he knew that there was no time to be wasted. Far ahead on the horizon he could see a pink glitter which could only indicate a further sinking. The Jerry U-boats were still about. Hurriedly he seized the loud-hailer again and went to the bows.

'Ahoy up there,' he cried. 'Ahoy Captain SS *St George!*'

'Hello below yourself,' the merchantman captain's thick gravely voice came back out of the grey gloom. 'Nice job of work. What now?'

Andrews sensed Thirsk looking at him. He lowered the loud-hailer for an instant. Yes, what now? He had been too occupied with the task in hand to consider what he would do once he had got the tanker round. Was it back to Iceland to the protection of the island's defences, with every mile westwards taking him further out of the Germans' range, or dare he attempt to get the tanker's vital cargo of oil through to the Russians who needed it so desperately? He bit his cracked, bloodied lip. It would be easy to go back. No one would blame him. Indeed there might even be a gong in it for him if he could get the great ship and its cargo safely into port. But he knew, in spite of the little voice inside screaming warnings at him, that would be an Eastbourne decision – and he was finished with Eastbourne for ever. He put the loud-hailer to his lips again.

'Ahoy there, captain! I'm going to have a try for Murmansk – north of Bear Island and into the Barents!' he yelled, his voice suddenly strong and full of confidence. 'What do you think, captain?'

There was a moment's silence. Andrews could imagine the thoughts racing through the mind of the dark shape on the deck far above him. Then the thick voice roared.

'We like your looks, Wavy Navy. We think you'll get us through!'

'Holy straw sack!' Dietz coughed thickly, 'thank God, they've gone!' He moved as if he were about to rise, but Hartmann grabbed his arm firmly.

'Not just yet – wait a minute, Dietz!' he gasped, knowing that another five minutes of the gas and the man already sprawled out on the deck would be dead, 'just one minute...'

But Dietz had not been mistaken; the

destroyer was moving further and further away, the sound of its screws diminishing by the minute. Perhaps the Tommy thought he had sunk them; perhaps he was afraid that there were other members of the wolf pack lurking off the black mass of Bear Island. Whatever the British captain's reasoning was, he was definitely going and they were saved.

Hartmann took a last look at the officer-cadet stretched out on the greasy deck, his chest heaving in shallow gasps.

He would have to take a chance. Painfully he rose to his feet.

'Diving stations,' he croaked. 'Get in trim.'

No one moved except Dietz. Hartmann raised his voice, fighting the gas flooding the compartment from the shattered batteries.

'You heard me – diving stations.'

One by one the crew staggered to their feet. The bilge pumps went into action with a steady thump-thump. Wessels, the bearded engineer reported dutifully.

'Boat rising – one metre, two metres up.'

Hartmann standing by the periscope, his cap already spun round with the peak to the rear, could now see the poisonous fumes lying in a heavy mist on the deck. The ratings staggering through it, looked as if they were without lower bodies. The boat was surfacing.

'Up periscope,' he said hoarsely. The men in the control room stared at the periscope longingly.

'Up periscope,' Dietz answered.

Gradually the greased gleaming steel tube rose to the surface. Hartmann grasped the handles and pressed his face to the rubber head-rest. The water fell away and his vision was clear. Hurriedly he spun the glass eye around the horizon, while the crew waited tensely, their heavy silence broken only by Lüttjen's persistent coughing. Hartmann took a deep breath. Nothing in sight save for the black bulk of Bear Island.

'All right – *surface!*' he ordered.

Compressed air streamed into the tanks. The water rushed out with an obscene gurgling sound.

'Down periscope,' he rapped. The tube sank. He adjusted his cap and waited impatiently. Lüttjens still hacked away like some ancient broken asthmatic. He heard the familiar noise of the boat breaking surface, rocking as if punch-drunk from the long hours submerged under water. The hatch opened with a dull metallic thud. Suddenly there was an outburst of frantic coughing as the submariners sucked in the fresh air in greedy gulps. Hurriedly Hartmann clattered up the dripping ladder, followed by Dietz and Lüttjens, sucking in the blessed air frenziedly.

'Shut up,' he ordered and strained his ears, turning his head slightly to the wind, to try to pick out the sound of ship's motors. There was none. The petty officers began their reports.

'Port clear ... starboard clear ... Aft clear, sir!'

'Thank you!... Ventilate the boat.' Below the two fans whirled into action, as the diesels took over and the damaged electric motors were hurriedly switched off. 'And let the crew come up in small groups when they've completed their duties,' Hartmann added urgently.

'Ay, ay, sir.' Wessels snapped.

Hartmann allowed himself a moment's respite, forcing his greedy lungs to suck in the air at regulated intervals, fighting to control the noise in front of a careless Dietz, who was too far gone to care.

'All right, Dietz,' he snapped finally. 'Let's go and have a look at those batteries.'

When they reached the confused mess of the batteries, the electricians, faces covered in smoke masks, were already trying to put out the fire in number two battery, from which white, choking smoke poured. Hartmann flung a quick glance at the scene.

'Well?' he demanded quickly, 'what's the damage?'

Wessels shook his head.

'Not so good skipper. We're running out of distilled water to put out that number two so you might as well write it off and if we don't use salt water they'll really begin to burn now that they're getting oxygen.'

'So you mean,' Hartmann cut in, 'that we can't dive! Our electric motors have had it?'

Wessels nodded numbly.

'Thank you,' Hartmann said curtly. He turned to Dietz. 'Come on, let's get out of here and let the electricians get on with the job. Check they don't do more than fifteen minutes at a spell even with the masks on.'

The conning-tower was crowded with ratings, their heads bared to the night sky, completely oblivious to the biting cold. The officer-cadet offered Hartmann the safety belt attached to the conning-tower, but Hartmann declined it.

'Dietz,' he ordered, 'follow me! I want to talk to you.'

A little surprised, Dietz followed him

down the slippery ladder on the side of the conning-tower and on to the deck gun, where Hartmann took a precarious grip on the icy metal.

Beyond the pitch-black heights of Bear Island, the Northern Lights showed brighter than ever, shooting brilliant blue and orange rays into the night sky. By their light, Dietz studied his skipper's face, and he shivered, but not with the icy cold. He felt instinctively that he was in the presence of death.

'You realize the position, Dietz,' Hartmann broke the silence slowly, staring at the stark black outline of the conning-tower, 'Now that the electric motors are out?'

'Yessir. We can't dive.'

'That's it. We have escaped with our lives. Now we must decide what we shall do with them. What do you suggest?'

Although he knew before he said them that the words he would utter were the wrong ones, Dietz played his expected role in the grim little game.

'We could make for Norway, sir. Hammerfest – Trondheim – somewhere like that. They might be able to patch us up sufficiently for us to get back to Kiel under our own steam.'

'You mean coasting around Bear Island on

the surface, sticking close to the shore until we can raise the Fifth Air Fleet to give us surface cover back to some Norwegian port?' Hartmann prompted softly.

'Yes, sir,' Dietz replied, feeling the blood hammer in his temples with fury at the futility of it all. Why the hell didn't the bastard get on with it? Hartmann knew what he was going to do. He was a law unto himself. He was the stuff that the holders of the Knight's Cross were made of.

Hartmann did not speak for a moment. There was no sound save for the soft moan of the wind and subdued chatter of the ratings awed by their miraculous escape and the rare privilege of being allowed on the conning-tower.

'What did you do before the war, Dietz?' he asked.

'I was a student at Hamburg University, sir – comparative philology.'

'Do you know what I was?' Hartmann said, 'I was *der letzte Dreck* – the scum of the earth, a sailing cadet on the school-ship. Hell with sails we called it. Scrubbing decks with a tooth-brush, getting little more than a couple of hours of sleep a-day, eating trash that no self-respecting pig would have touched. I could have gone to university too

– I had the *Abitur**. But I didn't want to. I wanted that hell with sails. And why?' He turned from his contemplation of the island to stare directly at Dietz. 'Because I knew that this would come,' his hand swept round the bleak desolate horizon. 'And this is what my whole life is about.'

'I don't think I quite understand you,' Dietz said, embarrassed at the skipper's confidences.

Hartmann gave him a queer little smile.

'Of course, Dietz, you are a civilian at heart, and my family have been soldiers ever since the time of the Great Elector. How could you know? So, my dear Dietz, what will we do? We will return to our base? Of course, we won't! We shall stay here and fight.'

'Sir, sir!' the officer-cadet's voice suddenly cut in from the conning-tower. 'A message!'

Hartmann swung round. 'From whom?'

The officer-cadet stared down at the two officers, outlined starkly against the dawn sky, and wondered for a fleeting instant what they had found to talk about that could be worth risking their lives for like that; then he yelled:

*The German high school leaving certificate.

'From the Big Lion, sir! From Admiral Doenitz...'

'What the devil do you mean, man, they haven't come on shift?' Vice-Admiral Fox-Talbot thundered into the telephone, his face almost crimson with suppressed rage. 'Don't they ruddy well know there's a war on? That convoy has to be loaded on time!'

The dockyard superintendent was suitably apologetic.

'Of course, sir, they know that. But your Hull dockies are a funny lot, sir, and after all, it is Boxing Day.'

'Boxing Day!' the Admiral exploded. 'Boxing Day – why those damned dockers of yours will box us all into our graves one of these days! Superintendent, I don't know how you'll do it – and I don't damn well care. But I want every dockie of yours, who should be on shift, on duty, even if you have to scour every pub in Hedon Road to do so!'

'But we can't do that, sir,' the superintendent protested.

'You can, sir, even if you take every last policeman in Hull to do so. Goodbye!' Fox-Talbot slammed the phone down, just as his aide came in bearing the intercept.

'What now?' he snarled.

'Just come in from naval intelligence, sir.'

Vice-Admiral Fox-Talbot's rage abated suddenly; it was not often that he was honoured by a communication from the smart young men who staffed Room 39 at the Admiralty.

'Give it here, Jones.'

Picking up his simple steel-rimmed spectacles he focused them on the message. Slowly he read it aloud.

'ALL UNITS CONCENTRATE ON PASSAGE SPITZBERGEN – BEAR ISLAND. NO FURTHER ENEMY SHIPS TO PASS. BLOCK THE GATE. GOOD LUCK AND GOOD HUNTING. HEIL HITLER. SIGNED DOENITZ.'

For a long moment Vice-Admiral Fox-Talbot did not move, and the young aide stared down at him anxiously; then he handed the intercept back slowly.

'File it,' he said quietly, 'file the damn thing. The naval historians will need it one day for their record of how Convoy PQ 8 perished.'

DAY SIX: DECEMBER 27th, 1941

'Yon gate's not just the way into the Barents – it's the gate to hell or the graveyard.'

CPO Thirsk to Lieutenant Andrews.

Dawn broke on the morning of December 27th, 1941 with the fog rolling in from the dreary hulk of Bear Island to the south. HMS *Rattlesnake* plodded on grimly, her engines straining to the utmost, towing the massive bulk of the *St George* behind her.

CPO Thirsk yawned, rubbed a weary hand over his jaw and promised himself that when he went off-watch he would shave before he turned in. With the rest of the crew running around like a lot of bearded Dervishes, someone had to remind them that they were in the ruddy Royal Navy.

'Bear Island,' Lieutenant Andrews said, lowering his glasses. His face haggard and worn. To Thirsk's sympathetic eye, the young skipper seemed to have aged five years in the last five days. Andrews licked his chapped lips. '74° 28′ North, 19° 13′ East, lying some two hundred and sixty miles North North-West of North Cape, Norway,' he recited the figures he had learned by heart at King Alfred, 'and some one hundred and forty miles south of Spitzbergen. According to the lieutenant instructor it may be regarded as the meeting point of the Barents, Greenland and Norwegian seas – the most isolated island in the whole Arctic Ocean.'

'Ay that might be so, sir,' CPO Thirsk said heavily. 'But it's more than that, sir. Up yonder is the gate. Once we're through that, we can count ourselves lucky. A lot of good lads have bought it up there and a lot more will before this ruddy war's over. I've done it half a dozen times on the way to Murmansk and it's put years on me.'

Andrews chuckled. 'Now, come on Chief, it can't be that bad.'

'Ay, it is, sir. Yon gate's not just the way into the Barents – it's the gate to hell or the graveyard. You just wait and see.'

It was an hour later that it happened. They were cutting their way through soft, mushy ice, covering the sea like gigantic mush-rooms on an early-morning, fog-bound meadow. The wind had died completely. There was no sound save the thump of the engines and an occasional grinding as they forced their way through a patch of ice. In the uncanny silence the snap of the steering chain breaking sounded like the crack of doom itself. The helmsman fought the wheel as the *Rattlesnake* began to swing round out of control.

'What the hell's the matter?' Andrews cried, his heart beating furiously.

Behind them in the fog, the tow wire was snaking back and forth in violent gyrations. Hawkins stemmed his whole weight against the wheel and grunted:

'She won't answer sir – the bitch won't answer!'

Andrews sprang to his aid. Together they exerted their full strength, the veins standing out on their temples. Still the rudder did not respond. The voice-tube hissed.

'Get it, Erickson,' Andrews cried through clenched teeth, still not relaxing his hold.

Erickson picked up the tube and listened impatiently to the mournful Scottish voice of the ERA in charge of the engines.

'It's no use, sir,' he snapped, relaying the ERA's message, 'the chain's gone. We're out of control!'

'Oh shit!' Andrews cursed and relaxed his grip. The *Rattlesnake* swung round and lay broadside in the trough. Behind them the tow twanged and went slack again the next instant.

On his journey north from King's Cross, Andrews had studied the *Rattlesnake*'s mechanism; it wasn't something they had taught at King Alfred. He knew that the steering impulses from the bridge were carried aft by two great chains. He knew, too, that at regular intervals the chains had to be tightened by adjusting the turn-buckles which were part of the linkage, since they tended to slacken off during normal use. The job was part of routine port maintenance. Apparently it hadn't been done in Hull, or else the strain of the night's towing was having its effect.

CPO Thirsk came panting back up the bridge stiff-legged, his duffle-coat thrown carelessly over his red flannel underwear.

'I've been down to the engine-room, sir,' he reported, fighting to get his breath back. 'Cheerful Charlie Chester down there' – he meant the mournful Glasgow ERA – 'says the port turnbuckle is snapped and one of the steel rods is fractured.'

Andrews considered the news for a second, hiding his helplessness behind the thoughtful look he used to adopt at board-ing school when he had been asked a question by a beak and hadn't known the answer. As the *Rattlesnake* wallowed in the trough and the first anxious cries started to come across the fog-bound water from the *St George,* Erickson came to his rescue.

'Sir, we've got to get Cheerful Charlie to build a new turnbuckle.' He swung round on Thirsk, every inch the old fishing skipper who knew his bonus depended on a quick decision. 'Has the chain slipped off too, Chief?'

'Ay, Charlie, it's gone.'

Andrews absorbed the news. He knew vaguely what they meant. When the port turnbuckle had snapped, the slack chain would have fallen off the toothed semicircle of the rudder quadrant, located in the extreme stern of the *Rattlesnake* beneath a low wooden grating on the after deck.

'Sod it,' Erickson cursed. 'I thought as much.' He swung round on Andrews again. 'Sir we'll have to replace that chain too.'

Andrews' heart sank. The chain could only be replaced by men crawling into a space four foot broad and less than fourteen inches high. There, lying full length on their bellies, soaked by the icy waves, they would have to lever the heavy chain back into place. A job of that kind, he knew, would be bad enough in the calm and relative warmth of Hull harbour; but out here in the midst of the ocean, it was virtually asking the impossible.

'How long do you think the two jobs would take, Petty Officer?'

'About three hours. Cheerful Charlie isn't a bad worker despite the fact he's already crying stinking fish and rubbing his hands like a bloody old washerwoman. He'll have a new turnbuckle done in that time. It's the replacing the chain that'll be the sod, sir.'

Andrews nodded grimly.

'Yes, I know it. In this weather. All right, we'll have volunteers for a start–'

'Me, sir,' Erickson cut in. He gave a wry laugh. 'And I'll volunteer Hawkins here.'

'Petty Officer!' Hawkins protested.

'Why not Hawkins. You're almost a Yorkshireman. Big in t'body weak in t'head.' Erickson was serious again. 'We're the strongest, sir. We can stand the strain easiest.'

'All right, Erickson, you're on. But after that all of us take our turn. Nobody's going to stand working in that water for long. It'd freeze the balls off a brass monkey!'

'All of us sir?'

'That's right, Erickson. You heard correctly – me included.'

'Good for you, sir. All right, Hawkins,

don't stand there like one-of-each waiting for vinegar, let's get on with it!'

The two big men clattered down the ladder and ran across the swaying aft deck towards the teak-covered grill which was already beginning to take the first of the white water.

'Sir.' It was Thirsk.

'Yes, Chief?'

'What about the *St George?*'

'Oh damn, I'd forgotten about her.' Andrews swung round and stared at the bulk of the stricken tanker wallowing in the mist behind them. Together they presented a prime target for any lurking Jerry U-boat. Separated, one of them at least stood a chance.

'Look Chief,' he said hesitantly, 'with both of us crippled like this–'

'Shall I order the lads to break the tow, sir?' Thirsk interrupted, his face grim. 'It's the only way, sir. I'm sure they'll understand on the *St George* – *all* of them.'

'Thank you, Chief,' Andrews said quietly. Then his voice rose confidently. 'It'll only be three hours at the most and besides this fog'll cover us. Tell their captain to sound his sirens at regular intervals once he begins to drift out of sight. I know it's risky, but I want him to know that we're going to come looking for him as soon as those damned chains are repaired again.'

Five minutes later the *Rattlesnake* had cast off the tow and the *St George* had begun to drift. Ten minutes later she was lost in the thick mist. Now there was no sound in the grey sea save the steady hammering from the *Rattlesnake*'s engine room and the muffled noise of the *St George*'s foghorn.

'By the great whore of Buxtehude!' St Pauli Willi exclaimed joyfully as the fog parted for an instant and the long low bulk of the *St George* slid into view, stern-first. Hurriedly he swung the periscope round and before she vanished again into the grey clouds, he caught a glimpse of the great hole in her engine room.

'A Tommy – and completely out of control!' he yelled to the sweating attentive men crowded around him in the submarine's control room.

He clapped the twin periscope handles together with a gesture of triumph and rapped 'periscope down'. As it slid downwards with a slight hiss of compressed air, he swung round on the others, the strain of the last two hectic days in which he had torpedoed an estimated twenty-three thousand tons of enemy shipping forgotten.

'All right boys,' he said in the same nasal dialect they used themselves.

'That's it, our last target. Twenty-three thousand plus ten thousand. That's thirty three thousand. Enough to make even the Big Lion crack his sour mug into a smile, eh?'

There was a low rumble of laughter from the men. Doenitz did have a very sour face at the best of times.

'All right, lads, no more torpedoes. So this job we'll do with the deck gun, eh? It'll be easy. That Tommy up there,' he jerked a fat thumb in the direction of the surface, 'is as good as dead. And then, lads, back to the Homeland. Tin for the lot of you – and after that the Reeperbahn.' He put his arm around the boat's Moses, a fresh-faced seventeen year old from Blankenese, who was vainly trying to grow a beard. 'The *Grosse Freiheit** and the *Herbertstrasse* so that our friend's beard here starts to sprout, eh?'

The veterans guffawed and the Moses blushed.

*A well-known night club. *Herbertstrasse,* the brothel area of Hamburg.

'All right, action stations and prepare to surface!' St Pauli Willi pressed the action button; the siren started to scream.

The German shell struck the SS *St George* just behind the bridge, sending fist-sized red-hot fragments of steel hissing low over the littered deck. Number 7 fuel tank burst almost immediately and the oil went up in a blaze of flame. The tanker heeled under the impact of the shell. As the burning oil spilled out the after-deck became a mass of angry red flames. Within a matter of seconds the after look-outs had disappeared, screaming as their bodies were devoured by the fire. A hundred-foot long blow torch hissed down a gangway. Tongues of flame licked down through holes in the torn deck. Steel doors started to buckle outwards and with every movement of the ship, the burning sea of oil spread further. The crazied men, trying to fight it in the thick choking smoke, were steadily driven back.

'Flood it!' the Captain cried on the burning bridge where the steel plates were beginning to glow a deep dull-red. 'For Christ's sake – flood!' he screamed, as men blundered by him blindly, their lungs bursting, the tears pouring down their smoke-burned faces.

Peter Thirsk threw a glance at the temperature gauge. The red danger mark was swinging high. With his horribly burnt hands, the charred bones already visible through the bloody flesh, he turned the wheel, sobbing with pain as he did so. The steel rods rotated, even though they were already buckled by the searing heat. The worm gear turned painfully. The inlet valves opened to admit the icy sea. He sank to his knees with the searing pain, but still he didn't remove his hands from the burning hot wheel. He had to open those bloody valves, even if the sodding wheel tore the hands off him. It would be what his Dad would expect of him.

The water came a fraction of a second later, but not in the manner that Peter Thirsk expected. It poured through the bulkhead in a bubbling, angry stream and it was white hot. He screamed as it hit his body flinging him helplessly against one wall and then another, carrying him before it like a fly, dragging his feet from under him, boiling him alive. His screams drowned as it bore him to his death.

St Pauli Willi watched the great tanker die without any sense of achievement. In the bad years of the Great Depression, he had shipped as an ordinary seaman with the old Hapag Lloyd, and like any other merchant sailor he was still awed and overcome by the sight of a ship going down, even if it were an enemy one and he had been the direct cause of its destruction. Down at the gun, the crew, their faces black with powder burns, cheered mightily, as the flames from the SS *St George* rose thirty metres into the grey air, burning away the fog. But although he could understand their elation at their victory, St Pauli Willi felt a sense of anti-climax – even depression. Next to him on the bridge, manning the anti-aircraft gun, the Moses tittered and said:

'Well, that's that, sir. Next stop the Reeperbahn and the girls, eh?'

'Don't laugh, Moses,' the U-boat skipper answered a little sadly. 'It's not just a machine dying out there, you know. It's men.'

'Sir,' his second-in-command screamed suddenly. *'The oil!'*

A wall of flame was sweeping towards the surfaced U-boat, forced out of the sinking tanker by the water let in by Fourth Officer

Peter Thirsk. For one long moment, St Pauli Willi was rooted to the conning-tower deck. He did not know what to do. The flames were roaring towards his boat. There was no longer time to dive. The flames would be upon them in a matter of moments. There was only one way out. Over the side now and deep into the icy water, hoping that the oil fire was confined to the surface only. At the top of his voice, St Pauli Willi bellowed:

'Abandon ship – *for heaven's sake, abandon ship!... AND Sparks give our position.*' His words ended in a scream of agony as the flames embraced his big body with a more fervent passion than any of the Herbertstrasse whores he had loved all his life.

Dietz scrambled up the ladder on to the conning-tower, as they wallowed in the bay, vision reduced to a matter of metres by the thick fog from the island.

'Sir,' he gasped.

Hartmann looked round and dropped his binoculars angrily.

'Yes what is it?' he asked, trying to fight back the rage which had overcome him when he realized that the fog might spoil his chances of a great killing off the gate.

'Distress signal from the U-66,' Dietz said

urgently. 'Kapitänleutnant Schulze is abandoning ship.'

'*What?*'

'Yes sir. The message is garbled. But it looks as if they sank a tanker.'

'That flash of flame to the west.'

'Could be, sir. I was below. I didn't see it. Anyway, the flames must have caught their boat. All our operator picked up after that was a request for help. They can't be more than ten kilometres or so from our position now.'

'Help! We're crippled ourselves, Dietz, you know that.'

'But our diesels are all right, sir. We can cruise on the surface. In this fog, we should be quite sa–'

'Out of the question, Dietz,' Hartmann interrupted him bleakly. 'St Pauli Willi's had his day. It is the price he expected to pay for his tin and the girls in St Pauli. Now it's our turn.'

'But they're only ten kilometres away, sir,' Dietz protested.

'As far as I'm concerned they could well be ten hundred away. It's our turn now. We're the guardians of the gate and I,' he paused and gave Dietz a cold smile, 'and I want to extract the requisite toll from our

Tommy visitors.'

CPO Thirsk was kneeling in the dirt of the latrine praying. He had never prayed since the night before Jutland when they had been told by Beatty that they were going to engage the German High Seas Fleet. Then he had been afraid for himself; now he was afraid for Peter. Thus he prayed in the only private place in the ship, bent on his stiff knees in the stench of the latrine, with strips torn off the *Daily Mirror* and *News of the World* stuck on a nail parallel with his eyes, fumbling over the half-forgotten words beaten into him in his backstreet school many years before.

But when he heard the faint, metallic boom – a sound like that made by his mother beating the side of their tin bath-tub to call him into the kitchen for his Friday night bath as a kid – he knew instinctively what it meant, and he rose from his knees with a wild cry of despair on his lips.

Erickson, his great chest heaving with effort as he stripped off his icy, soaked clothes and tried to find something dry, stopped dead when he heard it, feeling the small hairs at the back of his neck rise. It was a cry he would remember for the rest of his life. Thirty years later, when he had long abandoned England, he would tense in the midst of the brittle chatter, the fancy drinks, the soft luxury and remember that moment on the swaying tug lost in the Arctic and hear again that atavistic cry of despair and loss. And as the years passed, the Chief's cry came to signify for the ex-trawler skipper more than Thirsk's loss; it began to mean the loss of a whole generation – a way of life.

For when Thirsk came out of the latrine, buttoning his duffle-coat, his knees stained black from kneeling on the wet floor, his face was blank and expressionless. He blundered past Erickson still dripping icy sea-water, as if he were not there, a walking dead man.

'For Christ sake, Sparks!' Andrews gasped, as yet another wave crashed on to the teak lattice above them and swamped them with icy water, 'don't let go again!'

Sparks shook his head desperately to free his face from the water streaming down and blinding him.

'I'm doing my best, sir,' he choked. 'My hands is like sodding blocks of ice!'

'I'm sorry, Sparks,' Andrews said. 'I

know… Come on, let's have another go.' He thrust the long steel bar under the chain's heavy slippery link, towards the radio man.

'I'll count to three,' Andrews gasped, 'and then we'll heave together. Got it?'

Sparks nodded numbly, teeth chattering violently with the freezing cold. The two of them, joined by a life-line to the bridge, were lying face-down under the wooden grille which was about a foot above their soaked heads. Erickson and Hawkins before them had managed to secure the slipped chain to the side of the quadrant before they had been dragged back along the heaving deck exhausted, their hands frozen into immobile claws. Now it was their task to complete the job. They had to raise the heavy, slippery chain the last few inches and slip it over the top of the toothed semi-circle of the rudder quadrant, in the intervals between the icy waves which swamped them and would have swept them overboard, but for the wooden grille overhead.

'One – two,' Andrews counted, his whole body shivering in the intense cold – '*three!*'

With a mighty grunt, the two men lying flat on their bellies, heaved. But Andrews had misjudged once again. In that same instant, a great wave crashed on to the deck above them. Andrews just had time to cry:

'Hold it, for Christ sake, hold it,' when the tumbling water swamped them and they were choking for breath.

It was over in a matter of seconds, but to the two young men battling for their lives, it seemed that they were thrashing in the churning water for an eternity. Then it receded with a sullen hiss and they were left gasping there like fish. Yet despite his exhaustion and panic, Andrews' heart gave a great leap as he saw that Sparks had not relinquished his hold.

'Good for you, Sparks,' he cried. 'Come on, let's have another go – *quick!*'

'Right, sir … let's make it this time … I'm buggered…' His words came in hectic gasps as if his lungs were giving out for good.

'Take hold!' Andrews thrust the steel bar up under the thick link and grunted. 'Now – *lift!*'

The link began to edge upwards.

'It's moving,' Andrews yelled, the veins standing out on his temples with the strain, his face crimson. 'Don't let go, Sparks … for Chrissake, don't let go!' Sparks put his last strength into it, gasping like an asthmatic. The link moved another inch. Below him Andrews felt the *Rattlesnake* heel to port slightly. He knew what that meant. The next wave was on its way.

Summoning up the last of his strength, he heaved. His knuckles caught the gnarled side of the rudder quadrant. The metal ripped away the flesh. He yelped with pain. But he did not let go. At his side, Sparks was crying:

'Jesus ... Jesus ... Jesus ... let it go on, Jesus!'

Above the laboured sound of their breathing, Andrews could hear the vicious hush of the wave as it rolled nearer, gathering strength every instant, ready to crush them into nothing. He redoubled his efforts, feeling the muscles of his back and arms scream out in protest.

'Come on, come on,' he yelled. And then as the great wave swamped them and the steel bar was ripped out of their hands to tumble to the deck, the chain slipped over the quadrant and they were fighting for air underneath the grille. They had done it.

Half an hour later the Scottish ERA had finished tightening up the turnbuckle and Erickson at the wheel had executed the tricky manoeuvre of swinging the *Rattlesnake* off before the wind in the ever-mounting following sea.

He turned towards Andrews.

'The course, sir?' Andrews, still shivering with cold in spite of the rum and dry clothes, answered:

'The *St George* – we'll look for survivors.'

'Ay ay, sir. Survivors, sir,' Erickson's voice rang out confidently, but he dared not look at the silent CPO Thirsk standing at the side of the bridge; for he knew there would be no survivors. After all the *St George* had been a tanker, and tankers did not have survivors.

Fighting steadily mounting seas, which indicated that a great storm was brewing, but which did at least clear the fog, they pushed on towards the last position of the *St George*. CPO Thirsk stared out of the glass, as if he were a passenger admiring the heaving wilderness of the sea.

And then they started to plough their way through the dead: floating high on the surface like dead fish in a nauseating slick of blood and oil; shrunken black pigmies, charred like burnt meat and reduced to half their size by the fire split open from crotch to chin, gutted as neatly as the herrings most of the crew had worked with before the war.

Retching drily, Andrews forced himself to

look at the dead in the knowledge that they, too, were part of his education in the art of war. But to his right, CPO Thirsk stared at the bodies being tossed back and forth by the waves as if they were creatures from another planet.

Erickson reduced speed and the *Rattlesnake* nosed its way through buckets, empty shell-cases, steel helmets, smoke-floats, shattered scorched life-boats, life-belts, mockingly empty, while the crew clung to the railings grimly and stared down at the debris of the *St George* in shocked silence. There was nothing but death everywhere. The former fishing skipper threw a quick glance at Thirsk and then looked at Andrews inquiringly. Andrews indicated with a nod of his head that he should continue the search. Erickson took the ship into the wind carefully. The storm was mounting by the minute and he had had enough experience of Iceland before the war to know what was coming. Time was running out. Soon they would have to make a break for it and seek the shelter of Bear Island unless they wanted to end up like the poor devils bobbing up and down in the angry water below.

'Chief, I think the *St George* must have

gone down as soon as she was hit,' Andrews said gently.

CPO Thirsk standing near the window answered unemotionally:

'Yes, it would look like it, sir.' But he did not turn to face Andrews.

They continued their fruitless search for survivors for another thirty minutes. The sea was becoming wilder and more threatening every second, and Andrews was just about to give the order to turn about when ahead of them a column of white water shot into the air. In its centre it bore a dead man, his arms and legs whirling in the water, as if he were still alive. For what seemed a very long time the dead man hovered there above the sea, held aloft by the fountain of water, as though he were cursing them for venturing into this place of the dead. Then as suddenly as it had appeared, the corpse fell back into the boiling sea and vanished for good. CPO Thirsk, still standing at the window, began to sob.

Two hours later the elements had gathered all their strength for the great attack on the old tugboat. The anemometer on *Rattlesnake*'s bridge went crazy. The wind-speed needle flickered across the dial until it was registering gusts of up to ninety miles an hour.

The wind screamed across the white, heaving water. Sometimes, as she crested a wave, the *Rattlesnake* seemed to be standing on her stern, her bows pointing towards the threatening sky. Then she would teeter on the crest, hesitate and dive shuddering into the trough beyond, her screws exposed, threshing wildly.

There was chaos below. The ship's planks had worked loose so that the water was gushing in between them in swelling gouts, hissing as it came in contact with the red-hot boilers in the engine room. In the crew's quarters the tin mugs and canteens careened back and forth across the soaked deck. The great seven pound tins of plum jam crashed down, spilling their sticky contents over the playing cards that had fallen from Bunts' bunk.

Even some of the old hands could not take it. They lay in their heaving bunks, the dirty grey blankets drawn over their heads, attempting to blot the howling nightmare out while others clung to what they could find, their eyes wild with fear as every seam of the tiny ship groaned with the strain.

On the bridge, Andrews and Erickson

fought back with the desperation of men who knew that if they relaxed for one instant, they would be lost. Faces haggard and worn, eyes sore from peering into the icy wind, muscles screaming in protest against the strain, they battled with the storm. The normal world seemed aeons away. The only reality was the screaming wind and the icy, mountainous sea.

At one point the cook struggled up to the bridge. He hadn't shaved for days and he stank of grease, stale food and sweat. But in his hands, black with soot, he bore sandwiches made of biscuits and thick wedges of corned beef, covered in thick fat. To Andrews and Erickson, who had not eaten for over fourteen hours, they looked better than any food they had ever seen in their lives before. They grabbed them eagerly. Andrews yelled a curt, 'Thanks cookie', to the dirty rating and stuffed a whole sandwich in his mouth greedily, the fat dribbling down his unshaven chin.

Soon after that the gale rose to a fresh paroxysm of fury. As the wind struck them like a bludgeon, the *Rattlesnake* shuddered from bows to stern. Every timber, every rivet, every plate in the tug shook with the strain. She sank lower and lower into the madly heaving sea as ton after ton of water crashed over her. Erickson, madly fighting the bucking wheel, began to lose hope. In that raging ferment, no man nor boat had a chance. It couldn't be much longer before the *Rattlesnake* went under for good, and all of them with her. But the storm stopped as dramatically as it had started. At one moment the wind was howling furiously at nearly 100 mph, the next it had gone. The sea was as calm as it had been that morning, and the soaked, deathly pale ratings were wandering dazedly through the ship, trying feebly to bring some sort of order into the chaos above and below decks.

As twilight fell HMS *Rattlesnake* sailed through a still sea towards the sombre black outline of Bear Island. After the storm even Bear Island and its steep black cliffs seemed a snug harbour. At least the Northern Lights flickering across the mile-wide expanse of still black water created an illusion of welcome.

While Hawkins managed the wheel, Andrews lounged on the rail next to an exhausted Erickson. He contemplated the view with the complacency of a man who knew he had done a good job of work and deserved a rest. He ran his blood-shot eyes idly over the cliffs and gazed at yellow streamers of the Northern Lights illuminating their stark heights. Besides him, Erickson puffed at a damp Woodbine which refused to burn properly. Down below he could hear the cook raking furiously at the galley. Cook had promised that once he had managed to get the fire started again, he would run up a quick corned beef stew with suet dumplings. It was a tempting prospect and Andrews' stomach was already rumbling. They would heave to for the night in the shelter of the bay, check the ship properly for any serious damage after they had eaten and then in the morning he would radio the authorities for further orders. The convoy was gone. He had done his best. Now it would be up to Vice-Admiral Fox-Talbot to decide what should be done with HMS *Rattlesnake*.

But as he scanned the bay he glimpsed something which drove all thoughts of rest from his mind.

'Erickson,' he said suddenly, 'give me your night glasses – quick!'

Alarmed by the sudden urgency in his voice, the Petty Officer flicked the damp Woodbine overboard, although he well knew that it was forbidden to do so.

'Here you are, sir.'

Andrews grabbed them. The darkening bay swung into focus. There was no doubt about it. Against the flickering yellow background of the Northern Lights, a dark shape was silhouetted in stark relief. A submarine, and the only submarines in these remote waters were German ones. Wordlessly he unslung the glasses and handed them to Erickson, indicating the direction in which he should look. For a moment Erickson remained silent, then he whispered slowly:

'Christ Almighty – a Jerry sub!'

He stared at Andrews. The officer spoke in a whisper too.

'Yes, and we've got him trapped. To get out of this bay, he's got to pass us.'

'What are we going to do?'

'First thing, Erickson, get down below and tell the crew that if anyone as much as' – he hesitated over the word for a fraction of a second – '*farts,* I'll have the hide off him. All lights to be doused – and the cook can forget the corned beef stew this night. And then tell the Chief I'd like to see him on the bridge at the double.'

'But what are we going to do, sir?'

'What are we going to do?' Andrews echoed, his voice growing stronger as the great plan began to form in his mind. 'Why there is only one thing we can do, Erickson – sink her.'

DAY SEVEN: DECEMBER 28th, 1941

'What are we bloody well waiting around here for? When we're gonna bugger off back home to Hull?'

Bunts to Sparks

The wind came from the east. It was a bitter wind, scudding in straight from the ice-cap, turning everything white before it. As they crept through the night towards the unsuspecting U-boat, it grew steadily in strength, a wild virago, shrieking through the rigging.

But Andrews, peering into the darkness towards the stark outline of Bear Island, was happy with the bitter wind, especially since the Northern Lights were beginning their usual spectacular performance over the island itself. It would cover the noise of their approach. He glanced down at the men tensed at the guns. Spray and spindrift were washing over the *Rattlesnake* continuously, freezing everything and everybody under a thin film of sparkling hoar frost. If their mission had not been so serious, Andrews might have thought the scene beautiful, a Victorian sailor's Christmas card. But there was nothing festive about the gleaming gun barrels trained on the German submarine.

'Chief,' he called to Thirsk at the other end of the bridge, his night glasses glued to his eyes, peering into the night. 'Can you see anything?'

Chief Petty Officer Thirsk lowered his glasses deliberately. Since the death of his son on the *St George* he seemed to do everything laboriously, without any of his old regular Navy fire. It was as if he had suddenly admitted he was an old man, who should really be sitting at home, in front of the fire in his slippers.

'No sir, the Jerry's alone,' he replied tonelessly.

'Thank you, Chief, but keep your eyes peeled.'

Below, the crew prepared for action. Erickson checked the firing mechanism of the Oerlikon to ensure that it had not frozen, while Sparks smeared special winter oil across the sights to prevent them clouding over at the critical moment. Hawkins who was to man the twin Brownings on the monkey island breathed hard on his spray-frozen fingers to thaw them out again before placing his hands back in the thin gloves he wore to fire the machine-guns. Cass, the only other regular Royal Navy man besides Thirsk, manned the PAC rockets. He was a 'stripey', a three-badge man of forty odd, who had been in the Navy since he was fourteen and had still not qualified for a leading seaman's rating. But all the same he was completely reliable. Slow of speech, slow to protest, he merely remarked:

'Ah well, if the bugger starts flying, I'll get him down, sir.'

Bunts, as usual, had done nothing but grumble when he had been assigned to the Holman projector.

'You can't be serious, sir!' he had said contemptuously when he had been detailed off. 'What am I supposed to do with that sodding hot potato cart – lob the Jerries hot ruddy suppers?' But at that moment, at least, he was happy, warming his hands on the stove-like pipe through which the steam pressure from the engine room, used to fire the Heath Robinson gadget, was flowing, while the tins containing the hand grenades lay scattered all around him. Andrews, who had learned in these last terrible days that he had a gift for summing up men quickly, told himself that Bunts would always find a way of coming out top the sallow-faced Yorkshireman was a born survivor. They were now less than three miles away from the sub, clearly outlined against the back of the flickering lights as it rode unsuspectingly at anchor. On both sides, Andrews could make out the points of the little bay where they met the dark expanse of the ocean. They had the German trapped. He guessed that her present anchorage was too shallow for her to dive and escape. Her only chance now was for her to dive straight at *Rattlesnake* and make a crash dive as soon as she was in deep enough water, hoping that her unknown attacker did not carry depth-charges, which the tug didn't.

But Andrews was not going to give her that chance. He picked up the voice tube, instinctively lowering his voice, as if the Jerry look-outs might be able to hear him above the roar of the wind.

'Engine room,' the Scottish ERA's mournful voice floated up to him.

'Captain here,' Andrews said unnecessarily. 'Give me just enough power to keep out of the wind. I don't want the Jerries to hear the engines.'

The ERA who was a slow thinker seemed

to take an age to reply:

'Ay skipper, I'll do my best.'

They were getting closer to their target now. He could see the stark outline of its gun and conning-tower quite clearly whenever the wind let up and his eyes stopped streaming tears. Thirsk walked over to him. They were well within the bay; there was no more danger to be faced from outside interference. For a while they stood there in silence, side by side, observing the U-boat.

'They're wicked things sir, yon U-boats – loathsome things. It'll be a pleasure to sink her,' said Thirsk suddenly. Andrews looked searchingly at the Chief. But there was no emotion on his haggard old face.

'Yes, I suppose you're right, Chief. It will be a pleasure – a great pleasure.'

Andrews sucked his teeth which were beginning to ache in the icy wind. He could understand the Chief's words. He and his kind had hunted the U-boats in two wars, spending hundreds of nights in fear and anger, helpless more often than not as the lean grey wolves of the sea massacred the merchantmen. To see the U-boat anchored in the bay now must, for him, be like a policeman coming upon a long-wanted criminal, taking his ease at his own hearth.

He could comprehend the Chief's feelings that the submarines were wicked, loathsome things.

All the same, over there, across the couple of miles of sea still separating the two enemies, there was perhaps another young man like himself, possibly more efficient, better trained and harder, but who had the same doubts, the same fears, caught up in the dreadful mechanics of war.

'What's he like?' He asked himself, 'my Jerry?' Andrew Andrews had never met a German in his life and he wondered whether the U-boat skipper would be like the captains in the films. A gross bemonocled Prussian like Erich von Stroheim? No, too old. Lean sardonic and utterly ruthless like Conrad Veidt? No, he'd be out too. You couldn't be so cynical and still captain a U-boat. His Jerry would be like himself, he knew that instinctively, a young man fated to die in the next few minutes – and he, Andrews, would never even see him.

'Sir,' it was Erickson on the Oerlikon. 'We're in range now, sir.'

Andrew Andrews took one last look at the U-122 through his glasses and thought of that young German captain for a fleeting moment; then he yelled:

'Prepare for action!'

It seemed strange to Lieutenant Dietz that these harsh waters could produce such an awe-inspiring spectacle as the Northern Lights. Ignoring the ocean, he turned to watch as the first faint white fingers groped their way over the edge of the sheet black cliff before stabbing the dark sky like the flak searchlights back in his native Hamburg. As he watched, the night sky below them became a kaleidoscope of brilliant patterns.

'All the same,' he told himself, as he stamped his feet on the gleaming white deck of the conning-tower, 'they can have the Northern Lights any day. Give me old Petersen's *Kneipe* off Dammtor Station and a good hot glass of grog and you can bury me happily.'

He looked down at his watch and yawned. He still had another hour to go before he came off watch. It would be good to crawl into the oil-stained mess of his bunk and blot out Bear Island, the Arctic, Hartmann and the whole rotten war for four hours – if he was lucky. He shivered with the cold and glanced around the gleaming white conning-tower. The look-outs, their heads buried in the hoods, were alert enough despite the icy wind. He looked towards the sea; but it was dark, silent, and empty. He grunted. Hartmann was barking up the wrong tree. The Tommies – what were left of them – had already passed through the gate into the Barents. The U-122 was wasting its time. They would be damned lucky if they had another kill.

Time passed slowly. Over the cliff, the Northern Lights began to fade away, thickening the gloom. Dietz felt his head start to nod. Hurriedly he commenced working out one of the old derivations, working from the proto-Germanic as Professor Hackebeil of the old comparative philology institute had taught them to do in his seminars. He had just got from *Kaninchen,* cognate 'coney', to the modern English 'rabbit' when he was awoken by a blinding flash and his body catapulted upwards to smash against the periscope standards. His back was broken at once. For a long moment the spattered corpse hung between the standards, arms outstretched in helpless crucifixion. As the alarm bells commenced their wild frenzy below, the body of Leutnant Arnold Dietz *cand phil Hamburg* who with a bit of luck and no war, might have lived his life out, teaching languages in some shabby suburban Gymnasium slipped down slowly to the littered, blood-slicked deck. The battle had begun.

'Bearing green three-oh ... sub,' Andrews yelled as the smoke cleared to reveal that their first all-out salvo had well and truly peppered the U-boat's superstructure. 'Range one thousand... Deflection – zero!'

Erickson repeated the instruction at the top of his voice, as if he were aboard a battleship and not on a scruffy little ocean-going tug, which had been reclaimed from the scrap yards.

'Fire!'

Again all guns which could be brought to bear opened up. The staccato force shook the bridge. The 20mm shells poured out of the Oerlikon. The red tracer shells chased each other frenziedly across the water, drawing a glowing shadow behind them. The steaming yellow cartridge cases tumbled on to the gleaming deck, melting a great ring of ice around them.

On the monkey island Hawkins joined in with his twin Brownings. The green and white slugs ripped along the side of the submarine. Even at that distance the men on the bridge could hear them strike home.

On the U-boat's deck, men were crumpling into shapeless heaps. Others ran back and forth across the littered deck, shouting and waving their arms, whether in anger or surrender, Andrews watching the firing through his night glasses, could not tell.

One German sailor swung the Schmeisser machine-pistol he carried slung round his neck, to the front and loosed a vicious high-pitched burst in their direction. The tracer stitched the night. Bullets pattered against the metal sides of the bridge like heavy summer rain. Andrews ducked fearfully. Behind him on the monkey bridge, Hawkins did not duck in time. The twin Brownings jerked upwards as he slumped against them before pitching to the deck. Even above the thump-thump of the Oerlikon, Erickson heard the big man's dying scream. He pulled Sparks to the gunner's seat.

'Here, Sparkie, get on this. I'm going to get that bastard Jerry!'

He sprang over the dead Londoner, skidded along the icy deck and then catching himself in time, was up and behind the Brownings. The first burst almost cut the lone German sailor in half, flinging his body against the scarred side of the conning-tower. The Oerlikon joined in seconds later, pounding the U-boat's deck until metal scars appeared like the symptoms of some horrible skin disease and blood ran down the gleaming-hoar-frost deck, sluicing into the scuppers. Even at that distance, Andrews felt he could smell the stench of fresh blood, mingled with the acrid fumes of cordite and burning oil.

'Cease fire!' Andrews yelled, fearful that they might be using too much ammo and already waiting for the U-boat's reaction; surely, its skipper would be ready to surrender now with his boat's upper deck littered with dead and dying.

'Watch 'em, sir,' Thirsk warned sternly, 'They're a cunning lot, the Jerries, sir.'

For what seemed a long time nothing happened, while the echoes of the firing died away in the bowl of the black cliffs. Above Andrews, Erickson changed his belts hastily. Sparks yelled across to Bunts, who still kept his hands clasped around the warm steam pipe:

'Bunts, double off and get me some more ammo! I'm running out, mate.' Grumpily Bunts rose to his feet. 'Yeah,' he sneered, 'larking around like a daft kid, you are. All you sparkies are the same – all want to be sodding heroes–'

He stopped suddenly. A man had begun to clamber cautiously out of the conning-tower. In his hands he held what looked like a shirt or a vest. Very deliberately, as if he were afraid that it might not be seen, he commenced waving the shirt back and forth. A great howl of triumph went up from the men on the icy deck of HMS *Rattlesnake*.

'By Christ, sir,' Erickson yelled across at Andrews, 'the Jerry bastard has surrendered!'

Andrews fought back his elation.

'Wheel amidships,' he ordered in a calm businesslike voice. 'Stop engines. Stand by to board her!' As the bells clanged, he raised his voice and shouted to the men on the guns. 'Keep your eyes peeled. You never know, lads.' But he knew in his heart, there was no further need for concern. The Jerry submarine was well and truly beat.

Down below in the U-122 Hartmann wiped away the blood dripping from the body of the dead man slumped next to Dietz's grotesquely twisted corpse.

'Get ready,' he rapped, noting as he spoke, the wild-eyed looks of fear on the faces of most of the men in the U-boat's smoke-filled interior. 'Stand by to fire!' Up above, the officer-cadet, his limbs visibly trembling, still waved the flag of surrender. The boy was turning out braver than he had thought; he knew he was letting himself in for an Ascension Day mission* whatever way things turned out.

Hartmann licked his dry lips. His hands were steady again now. He had recovered remarkably quickly from the surprise of the sudden attack. God, if that Dietz were still alive, he would have him court-martialled for his damned negligence! But it was too late to worry about that now. They must get out of this terrible trap. He raised his hand. The wizened petty officer at the end of the boat nodded. The torpedo men were ready.

'Fire one – fire two!' Hartmann yelled.

The U-122 rolled with the shock of the recoil. The officer-cadet continued waving the flag above his head in the open hatch. The boy knew that the last moments of his life were racing away, but he dared not duck. The boat was blind without him. He would have to report the torpedoes' run. But once the Tommies spotted them, they would bring the full weight of their

*German expression for a mission without return.

firepower to bear on the conning-tower.

Hartmann swung round on the mesmerized crew, tensely waiting to know whether the surrender ruse had worked or not.

'You, you, and you,' he ordered, 'get ready to follow me topside, with your weapons! You lot,' he rapped at the group of sweating ratings around the little Hamburg petty-officer, 'stand back as a gun crew. Obermaat, you're in charge!'

Hartmann flung a glance at his watch. Five seconds had gone. Above him the officer-cadet was waving his flag frantically. Still the Tommies suspected nothing.

'Sir, the officer-cadet screamed, 'we've miss–' His words ended in a burst of automatic fire, as the British realized they had been tricked. The officer-cadet slammed against the side of the conning-tower, remained half-standing for a fraction of a second and then tumbled head-first down the ladder, his face a bloody pulp.

'Wessels,' Hartmann yelled frantically, 'both engines full astern!'

The engines roared. Men were dashed against the inner bulkheads as the U-122 sprang backwards, hitting the rocks beneath the water. Sparks flew and thick fumes belched into the stern from the exhaust. But the angry British fire hissed harmlessly over their deck.

'Both engines – full ahead!' Hartmann bellowed. 'Follow me the men with the weapons – and that guncrew!'

As the U-122 shuddered, strained to get off the rocks and then shot forward, Hartmann kicked the dead cadet's body out of the way and scrambled up the blood-soaked ladder. The rest swarmed after him, jolted from side to side as the boat was struck by another burst of British fire.

The deck was a red mess of dead ratings sprawled in careless heaps. Less than a kilometre away a small squat boat – it could not be more than six hundred tons' displacement – was firing at them all out. In an instant, he took in the fact that the Tommies did not have heavy weapons. All the damned same, the air was filled with the bitter chatter of automatic weapons and the maniac scream of ricochets off the bridge.

'Midships!' he bent to bellow down the hatch, past the heads of the waiting gunners.

The engineer officer reacted at once. The boat swung round. It was a dangerous thing to do. But the manoeuvre caught the

Tommies off guard. Hartmann did not waste the opportunity granted him by the respite.

'Gunners on deck,' he roared urgently.

They came scrambling past him, dropping over the side of the conning-tower which was protected from the British fire. A man missed his footing on the slippery deck and plunged overboard. But no one had time for him. He disappeared a moment later in the U-122's churning white wake.

While the crew under the wizened little PO tried to ready the gun, the icy metal tearing the skin off their hands as they did so, Hartmann pulled a Schmeisser from the hands of a dead sailor.

'Fire,' he yelled. 'In heaven's name – *fire!*' He fired a wild burst at the British ship which had now started its engines again and was heading towards them in a collision course. The others joined in. Tracer leapt across the churned water knitting momentarily with the British fire. 'Sweep her bridge – for Christ sake,' Hartmann screamed knocking up the machine-pistol of the man nearest him.

Twenty-millimetre shells from the enemy Oerlikon flayed the deck below. Two of the gunners reeled from the frozen gun, their twisting bodies splashed with fresh scarlet.

Next to him the tommy-gunners ducked as the 20mms raked the conning-tower. Thin red-hot slivers of steel hissed through the air. Behind him a man screamed and clapped a hand to his head, blood spurting through his tightly clenched fingers. Another dropped to the bloody deck without a sound. Hartmann's brain was working with electric precision. He had to act now. But what was the Tommy captain going to do? Was he intending to ram the U-122? No, that was hardly likely, save as an act of desperation: the Tommy was too small. He was coming for the kill with his guns, relying on the fact that until now the U-122 had not fired a single shot at him.

But what would the Tommy captain expect him to do now? Swing about and head for the open sea or at least far enough out for him to crash dive – the Tommy wouldn't know that he could not run under water because of the defective batteries. Suddenly Hartmann made up his mind. A rapid turn to starboard might just fool the enemy. The Tommy wouldn't expect such a manoeuvre. For a few moments the U-boat would be completely helpless as it swung round, broadside on to his bow. Then he would slice across the bay, crash dive as soon as the water was deep enough and stop all engines. What happened next would depend on whether the Tommy had depth charges or not. If he tumbled to the trick. Perhaps he would assume the U-122 had escaped out to sea.

He grabbed the voice pipe just as the submarine's gun spoke for the first time sending an erratic shot across the bay.

'Listen Wessels,' he yelled above the vicious chatter of the British Oerlikon as it poured a stream of tracer at the gun crew desperately reloading and adjusting their sights, 'when I give the order hard a-starboard, I want full power astern with your starboard engine, port full ahead. Understand? Wheel hard over and she should come around pretty well. Then give her all you've got with both engines – full ahead. As soon as we reach sufficient depth, crash dive.'

'Dive, sir – but the men on deck at the gun and the batteries,' the bearded engineer protested.

'Issue smoke masks. As soon as we're below, we'll stop all engines. As far as the men on the deck–'

A salvo of British shells ripped down the side of the conning-tower and drowned his words. At his side the metal glowed a dull red for a brief instant. On deck another member of the gun crew slumped down and a man from behind the conning-tower doubled to take his place.

'For God's sake, do as I say,' Hartmann shouted. 'Hurry – time's running out.'

'Ay, ay, sir.'

Hartmann took a last look at the Tommy. It seemed to his trained eye that the tell-tale humps of the depth charges were absent from her aft; he hoped so. Below the PO screamed 'fire' and another 57mm shell tore the sky apart to land harmlessly into the water 50 metres away from the Tommy. It was now or never.

'Hard a-starboard,' he yelled, straddling his feet instinctively to take the strain.

The boat swung round with a tremendous clatter. He grabbed the icy conning-tower as he was nearly flung off his feet. Behind the conning-tower a rating, taken completely by surprise, was flung overboard and disappeared in the wildly churning water. But the Tommies were caught off guard too. Their salvo fell a good sixty metres too short, peppering the sea purposelessly.

'Stop starboard!' he screamed down the voice tube. 'Full ahead starboard!'

Below, the engineer officer was sweating,

his eyes bulging out of his head as he watched the myriad dials waiting for the first one to indicate disaster. The U-122 swung around, leaving a huge white S in the water behind it.

'Both engines – ahead!' Hartmann yelled.

The tough little boat leapt forward, rapidly closing the gap between her and the surprised Tommy. Their faces came into focus now, not just white blobs but features recognizable in the red and white stabs of flame from the guns. Just behind the Tommy bridge, Hartmann could see a man swinging round a twin machine-gun.

'Knock it out,' he bellowed at the gun crew.

Sweat pouring down his face in spite of the biting cold, the PO feverishly swung the deck gun round. A fresh shell was rammed home. The breach swung closed with a clatter of metal on metal.

'Fire!' the PO screamed urgently.

As the British machine-guns began to stammer their message of death, the German cannon cracked into action. Its shell could not miss now at such short range. It tore away the Tommy's mast-head. The enemy ship reeled wildly, its funnel nearly touching the water. In that same instant Lüttjen's excited East Frisian voice cried through the tube.

'We've got the depth! Just! But we can risk it!'

'Colossal,' Hartmann yelled exuberantly. 'Stand by to dive, Lüttjens!'

'Ay, ay, sir!'

Below, the sirens commenced their shrill, urgent wail. Across the water the British ship had righted itself again. Its cannon were beginning to speak once more. It was time to get out of the way. Hartmann drew a great breath.

'Dive!' he yelled into the tube above the noise.

In that same moment, a hammerblow smashed his shoulder, and he felt a searing pain as he was hurled against the side of the conning-tower, all breath knocked out of him by the shell fragment. For an instant he could not move. Far away he could hear the screams of the alarmed gun crew as the bows of the U-122 began to sink rapidly and the white water swamped their position. Then something wet and warm was seeping through his thick layer of protective clothing and he awoke to his danger.

As the U-122 started to incline steeply and the enraged Tommy gunners, seeing their prey escape, stepped up their rate of fire, he forced himself erect. Staggering to the centre of the conning-tower, he dropped through the hatch to the deck below. Ratings sprang across his body and snapped the hatch closed with fumbling fingers. His clouded eyes could just make out that, for some obscure reason, the rivets were turning red. Then Leutnant Hartmann groaned and let his head fall to the deck. Darkness swamped him and the U-122 disappeared beneath the white waves of the little bay.

Twice, the German sailor struggling in the water still churning in the wake of the vanished U-boat, pushed away the boathook, screaming invective at Erickson balancing precariously at the swaying rail.

'Let the bastard drown, Petty Officer,' Bunts snarled, his hands still clasped around the heated steam pipe.

'Hold your mouth!' Andrews snapped angrily, fighting back his disappointment at having lost the U-boat.

'Well, I ask you, sir.' Bunts persisted, as Erickson made yet another attempt to rescue the only survivor of the abandoned U-boat gun crew.

'If you don't damn well shut your filthy mouth, Bunts, you're for it,' Andrews cried in exasperation. 'CPO. Watch that man. One more word from him and I want you to take his name!'

'Yessir,' Thirsk said.

'Petty Officer,' Andrews addressed Erickson, 'get the damned fool up will you! We can't hang around here much longer.'

Erickson needed no urging. His leg muscles, screaming with the strain of trying to hold himself against the heaving deck, would not stand much more. He swung the brass-tipped heavy boathook and hit the German struggling in the water below at the back of the head. He screamed with pain and stopped trying to avoid the hook. The next instant, Erickson had slipped it neatly under the hood of his coat and heaved.

'Give a hand somebody,' he grunted through clenched teeth.

Sparks and the three-striper rushed forward to help, while the German, dangling half-out of the water, struggled like an obstinate fish. Five minutes later they had him stripped off in Andrews' tiny cabin. He was trembling with cold despite the heap of blankets, and coughing after every sip of the mug of rum, which Erickson was forcing him to drink.

'All right, Erickson,' Andrews ordered when he was satisfied that the prisoner was capable of answering questions.

'Now, listen,' he addressed the prisoner, 'do you speak English?'

The little German looked up at the young Tommy captain in his dirty yellow duffle-coat and salt-stained sea boots. His face was exhausted, unshaven and haggard and there were dark circles under his eyes. The Tommy didn't look much different from that arsehole Hartmann, save for the eyes; they were wary, but not filled with the fanatical light that animated Hartmann's.

'Yes,' he said thickly, his lungs still filled with sea water, 'I am speaking English. I was sailing with the White Star line in the olden times, before I go to the – er *Kriegsmarine. Wie sagt man?*' he looked up at the three of them. 'How you say?'

'Navy,' Andrews volunteered and fell silent wondering what to ask next.

The ever resourceful Erickson did the job for him.

'How come your skipper abandoned you like that? Let you go when he went under?' he added when he saw the little German did not understand the word 'abandoned'.

The German's face creased angrily.

'Das Schwein, der Saukerl, das Arschloch,' he cursed until Andrews snapped:

'Speak English!'

'The swine!' the German snarled. 'He left us! Not a chance, did we have. But he will not escape.'

'What do you mean?'

The German coughed thickly. His lungs wheezed. Thin pale liquid trickled from the corner of his mouth. Silently Thirsk handed him a dirty white towel. The German accepted it gratefully and wiped his mouth.

'Get on with it,' Andrews snapped in his eagerness. 'What do you mean – your ship won't escape!'

'The motors, captn – the electric ones, they are kaput. He cannot sail underwater.'

'What?' Andrews exclaimed. 'What did you say?'

'I have just said – he cannot sail under the water.'

Andrews looked at Erickson in triumph.

'Did you hear that, Petty Officer? The bastard's still down there, somewhere in the bay! We've got a chance to get him. Quick. No time to lose. Get a double watch on deck. If he wants to get out of this, he'll have to come up and we want to be ready when he does. Come on – at the double!'

'Sodding corned beef and dog biscuits again!' Bunts grumbled. I thought that pansy of a cook had got the galley going again!' He dropped the sandwich on the stained mess table in disgust. 'I won't have any ruddy choppers left, if I have to go on eating that ket any more.'

'If you don't want it – give it here,' Sparks said.

'Put yer hand on that grub – and I'll have it off,' Bunts said threateningly.

Sparks laughed easily.

'Go on, Bunts. Yer always the same – always crying sodding stinking fish!'

Bunts looked around the crew's quarters where the off-duty men sprawled fully clothed on their beds, trying to keep warm in the ice-cold hold, their breaths fogging the air in little grey clouds.

'And who wouldn't cry stinking fish with this sodding lot!' he said bleakly. 'Me bollocks are nearly frozen off, the grub's not fit for our dog back home and we're wasting our time waiting for that sodding German sub to come up. Either it's slipped away or it's sunk. What are we bloody well waiting around here for? When we're gonna bugger off back to Hull?' He looked accusingly at Sparks. 'Don't you want to get back eh? Scared you'll find yer missus has got herself a Polish fancy man?' Sparks ignored him.

'Of course, I want to get back to Hull, you fond bugger!' he exclaimed. 'But that Jerry's still down there and the skipper wants to get him. It stands to reason.' Bunts took a bite of his sandwich and said disgustedly.

'Don't give me that bullshit! You're like the rest, Sparks – and I thought you had a bit more savvy than them silly sods. What do you want to be – a ruddy hero. If there is a sub down there and if we did manage to sink it, who the hell do you think would get a medal? Thee! Not on your nelly.' He took another bite of his sandwich and pulled a face, 'Na, you wouldn't get a medal – unless it were a putty one. That soft Mary Ann of a skipper would though.'

'Can't you ever put a sock in it,' Erickson's voice snapped from the head of the companion way. 'Ever since I've known you, Bunts, you've done sod all except but complain.'

'Well, it's serious, Petty Officer,' Bunts said, 'I knew the minute that git upstairs said F – O – X that nothing good would come of this cruise. The sooner the *Rattlesnake* is back in the bloody Humber, the better I'll be pleased. Every minute we fool around here, the more danger we're in.'

Erickson did not answer for a moment. He had been sailing from the East Coast ports long enough not to laugh at the old fishing suspicions. He remembered his father telling him the story of the old Staithes boat which had gone out although a crew member had used the word 'pig' after a few pints had loosened his tongue in the little fishermen's pub down at the quay. In spite of the fact that it was summer and the weather nearly perfect, the boat had capsized and virtually the whole of the village's adult male population had been drowned. How did you explain things like that? He knew he certainly could not.

'You may be right, Bunts,' he said hesitantly. 'But there's nothing we can do about it. Try to imagine yerself telling the Royal Navy that a ship better not go to sea because somebody used a certain word.'

'It's no skin off my nose, Petty Officer. All I know is that we'd better get our skates on and get off home as soon as poss.'

Erickson's face hardened. 'Ay, and all I know is that you'd better get yourself up to the skipper – he wants you.'

'Have a heart, Erickson. I've just come off

watch, you know. I'm entitled to my rest.'

'I know,' Erickson retorted. 'Now get up to the captain.'

Bunts face contorted into a sneer.

'Oh, I see, it's like that is it. Crap, said the King, and a thousand arseholes bent and took the strain, for in them days the word of the King was law.'

Erickson doubled his big fist.

'One of these days, Bunts, it's going to give me the greatest of pleasure to sort you bloody well out. Now get up there to the skipper. On the double, do you hear.'

'Sit down, Bunts,' Andrews said.

Somewhat surprised, the sailor took the cabin's only other seat.

'You can smoke, if you like.'

'I've no fags, sir … cigarettes, I mean.'

Andrews handed him a tin of fifty Capstan. 'Help yourself.'

He waited till Bunts had lit up, then he began. 'Now Bunts I know you don't have much of an opinion of the projector – neither do I really. It is a bit Heath Robinson, I must admit.'

Bunts did not understand what the skipper was talking about. But he said nothing. He had a fag, the skipper's cabin was fairly warm and so far he hadn't been asked to do anything dangerous. So he listened.

'But I'm wondering whether we could use it to locate that Jerry sub – even if we were lucky to force her to surface.' He paused and looked at Bunts expectantly.

'How do you mean, sir?'

'Well, I believe those grenades you use in the cans have a four second fuse.'

'They do, sir.'

'Well, my guess is that the Jerry can't be very deep. A four second fuse should reach for the thing to explode somewhere close to it – close enough.'

Bunts' first reaction was to cry – 'Have you gone off yer sodding nut?' But the angry words came out in a polite:

'But them hand-grenades wouldn't harm the sub, sir. Even if one of them exploded right on the Jerry's outer casing, he'd hardly notice it.'

'Naturally, I know that already, Bunts. But what if we bundled several grenades together so that there'd be a big enough bang for the Jerries to think that we're lobbing depth charges at them?' He looked at Bunts triumphantly.

Bunts' disgruntled expression did not change.

'But where would you find a tin big enough to put 'em into, sir?'

'I've already thought of that. CPO Thirsk is working on it with the ERA. Now PO Erickson tells me that you're a dab hand with the projector. Do you think that you can lob the things at regular intervals in the rough area where we believe the sub might be without damaging our own keel? It'd be rather like throwing stones into a pond close to yourself without getting your clothes wet.'

Bunts rose and stubbed out his cigarette.

'I don't rightly know, sir. But I'll do my best,' he conceded grudgingly. 'I'm not promising nothing, mind you.'

'I don't want you to, Bunts,' Andrews said appeasingly. 'All I ask is that you do your best. All right, you can cut along now and see CPO Thirsk. And tell Petty Officer Erickson, please, that I'd like to see him again.'

Bunts reached for his cap.

'Ay, ay, sir.'

While he waited for Erickson, Andrews sat on the edge of his rumpled evil-smelling bunk, and stared contemplatively at the picture of the dead skipper's mother. She was not much different from his own, save that his mother took a great pride in her figure and hadn't become so dumpy. His eyes fell on the bunk and he wondered what the dead skipper and all the other skippers who had slept in it over the last twenty odd years would do in his position. He had seen immediately what Bunts had thought of his scheme; the look in his eyes was obvious.

'Let's stop messing about,' it had said, 'and get back home.' And probably there were plenty more in the crew who thought the same.

In truth it would be easy to turn now and make for home. But somehow he thought the unknown men who had preceded him in command of the *Rattlesnake* would not have given in so easily. If, at that moment, anyone had asked Andrew Andrews what duty was, he would have been pressed to give an answer that made sense. Duty was something one did to respect a tradition that one had grown up with.

'All that red on the map,' his prep school geography teacher used to say. 'One third of the world – and it's ours.'

It was 'pater' (his mother had always insisted on that form of address for his father) slipping away gradually and miserably after the brief heroics of Zeebrugge, dying in a bathchair on a suburban lawn in Eastbourne. It was the long list of names on the 'Roll of Honour, 1914–1918' in the school chapel; Empire Sunday and the long jingling bemedalled ranks of middle-aged men and the even longer line of bathchairs and invalid carriages which followed them; it was the films – *The Lion Has Wings, In Which We Serve;* the crisp orders, the sound of the bugles, the stamp of heavy boots on early morning gravel – the feeling of belonging to something which was more important than oneself. It was that ill-defined feeling, more a kind of spiritual warmth, which made a man believe that it was worth sacrificing one's life for it.

Thus it was that when he answered Erickson's knock at the bulkhead outside his cabin, Lieutenant Andrews' voice had the confident ring of a man sure that he was doing the right thing.

Below, Bunts knew he wasn't.

'Do you know what the silly sod's going to do now?' he asked, as the crew cleaned their weapons and prepared for their last fight with the U-boat. 'He's gonna depth charge that sub up – if the bleeder's still there that is, *with hand grenades!*' He looked around at their heads bent over the weapons. 'I ask you, lads, have you ever heard owt as soft as that. And what the hell does it matter in the long run, anyway?' he continued bitterly. 'What's the lot of us doing out here? The Icelanders – the sods – couldn't care less. They won't even look at us sailor lads when we put in there. A whore in a taxi at thirty-five bob a jump – that's about all we ever see of them. And the Russkies ain't much better. No protection for us. The only thing there is that Judies is cheaper – a packet of tea and a tin of Capstan and they'll have their drawers down right sharpish for you. But that's all.

'What's the good of the whole bloody convoy lark anyroad? Once the trouble starts, the escorts take off and leave the merchant navy lads on their todd. And we all know what happens then. Believe you me, mates, it's allus us poor little blokes who have to carry the can back, whether it's peacetime or wartime – and all for what? For bugger all.'

But no one was listening. There was a job to be done. Speed was vital and they had no time to waste on Bunts and his kind. When that sub surfaced, they had to be ready for it. After a while Sparks leaned over from his bunk and said. 'Bunts, pass me the rifle oil from the table, mate, will you?'

'Get it yersen.'

Unoffended, Sparks rose and picked up the bottle.

'Tha's narked, Bunts,' he said, his eyes sparkling, as he went back to his bunk. 'Real narked, aren't you, Bunts!'

Hartmann slumped in the metal seat, while the crew stared at him in horror, whether because of his shattered shoulder or what he had done to the gun crew, he did not know – nor did he care. He felt numb and weakened by the pain. It throbbed and ripped at his shoulder, making thought almost impossible. But he knew he must not give in to it. There was the boat to be saved, and it was his duty to save it.

The rating with the Red Cross satchel slung over his shoulder looked at the gaping shrapnel wound aghast.

'I don't know whether I can manage that, captn,' he said. 'We only did superficial wounds at Mürwik.'

Hartmann forced a smile.

'Well, Dudeck, here's your chance to learn on a live guinea pig – and an officer to boot.'

Lüttjens pushed by him.

'Skipper,' he said, 'better let him give you a shot. I don't want to frighten you, sir, but that wound looks pretty bad.'

'You won't frighten me, Lüttjens.' He winced with sudden pain. 'And even if I accepted a shot,' he continued, his breath coming with difficulty, 'what then? Who would take over the boat?'

'Well, I would, sir,' Lüttjens said hesitantly.

'Of course – and what would you do then?'

Lüttjens licked his lips. For the first time Hartmann noted how thick the lower one was – the sure sign of a sensualist, whose primary concern would be his safety and self-indulgence.

'Well, sir, it's obvious what we have to do now, isn't it? We've had it! The electric motors are shot. That shitty Tommy is up there waiting for us to come up. It's only a question of time and then we'll have to come up!' He shrugged. 'Everyone knows what will happen then.' There was a soft murmur of agreement among the men at the back of the group, hidden from the wounded captain's view. 'So why don't we get it over with now and save ourselves more misery–' He glared down at Hartmann defiantly.

'By getting it over with, I presume you mean surrender, Leutnant Lüttjens?'

Hartmann hesitated. He knew he needed Lüttjens and the rest of them. He dare not push them too far, but he must make them want to fight on. Accordingly he fought back his anger.

'I understand what you mean, Lüttjens,' he said as calmly as he could, telling himself that the day of reckoning would come for Lüttjens once he had him back in Kiel. 'But all is not lost yet by a long chalk. Before we submerged, I saw that that Tommy did not have depth charges. So we are safe from him as long as we stay under the surface.' Painfully he raised his wounded arm to prevent any objection from the other officer, sweat breaking out over his forehead with the sudden agony. 'I know what you're going to say. But we won't have to stay below too long. The Tommies' bases are too far away for them to get anti-submarine craft or planes here quickly. We are more fortunate – our bases are in Norway. We are going to ask for air cover to get rid of that bastard up there and get us back to the nearest Norwegian port.

'It is strictly forbidden to break radio silence,' Lüttjens admonished, but Hartmann could see the light of hope dawning in his red-rimmed eyes. All around him there was a sudden excited mumble as the crew absorbed his words.

'I realize that, Lüttjens. But this is a number one emergency. Perhaps the Big Lion will only recommend the Führer to give you the Knight's Cross by itself – instead of all the salad dressing to go with it. Now then, Lüttjens, get that message coded at once. You,' he looked across at Dudeck, 'let's see what you can do, bone-mender. And no drugs to put me out. I want a clear head these next hours.'

DAY EIGHT: DECEMBER 29th, 1941

'Why not sit down now?… Let the young men fight the battle.'

German POW to CPO Thirsk

A high silver moon hung in the sky casting a spectral light on the still sea. The wind had died to a light breeze and HMS *Rattlesnake* hissed softly through the dark cold swell. Now the only sounds that disturbed the quiet were the deep throbbing note of the ship's diesels and the steady hammering of the ERA and his mate as they prepared the makeshift depth charges from lengths of pipe long enough to hold four grenades.

Andrews shivered in the coldness of the approaching dawn, reaching up stiff fingers to pull the collar of his dufflecoat tighter around his neck. How much longer would the ERA take? He'd been at it nearly all night. Time was running out. He must attack soon. He tugged at the end of his frozen nose and glanced at the helmsman. The old three-striper might have been carved from stone, as he held the *Rattlesnake* true to course.

Andrews scanned the dark water ahead. Nothing stirred. It was hardly possible to believe that down there somewhere, only a matter of a few fathoms below them, there was another ship, lurking, packed with men, who although they spoke another language, had the same fears, the same hopes, the same illusions, the same desires as they did; but whom they must soon kill because they bore the label – enemy.

Suddenly the hammering stopped below. Andrews who had been pacing the bridge restlessly came to an abrupt halt. He cocked his head to one side and threw back the dufflecoat hood so that he could hear better. The hammering did not commence again. The ERA and his mate were finished. It was the moment he had been waiting for all the long night. Urgently he strode to the voice pipe.

'Engine room.'

'Ay, sir,' the dour Scotch voice came floating upwards. 'Yon pipes are ready now. But they're nothing to write home about.'

'Good. Don't worry – as long as they force Jerry up to the surface. Stand by for action.' He swung round on the three-striper.

'Helmsman,' he snapped. 'Starboard fifteen. North by north-east.'

Erickson came running up on to the bridge, buckling on his steel helmet.

'You heard, sir?' he gasped.

'Yes, PO sound action stations, please.'

The loud, endless shrill of the alarm bells began all over the ship. Feet started to pound along the passageways. The ratings burst on to the deck, struggling into their outer clothing, tugging on their helmets as they took up their action stations.

'Oerlikon crew closed up, sir!'

'Brownings closed up, sir!'

'Holman closed up, sir!'

Andrews gave a swift glance about him, his heart beginning to thump with excitement. Fore and aft looked all right. The gun crews were alert and waiting. He couldn't see Thirsk – perhaps he was still down with the ERA – but Bunts, assisted by Sparks, was clearly outlined standing by the Holman.

'Action stations closed up, sir,' Erickson yelled from behind, as if he were a thousand yards away and not ten feet.

Below them the *Rattlesnake* started to tremble like a live thing, as she picked up speed.

'Very well, Bunts,' Andrews bellowed

above the increasing noise, 'begin operations – now!'

Utterly weary, CPO Thirsk pulled himself off the bunk as the alarm bells sounded and sat there for a moment, his grey head bowed. Opposite him, in Erickson's bunk, the little German started up in surprise, a look of terror in his eyes.

'Himmel, Arsch and Zwirn!' he cursed, *'was ist nun kaputt?'*

Then he realized where he was.

'Was this the alarm?' he asked the old man huddled opposite him. Thirsk nodded numbly and gazed at his false teeth which he kept in an old cigarette tin near his bunk. Somehow he didn't seem to have the strength to reach out and put them in.

The German raised himself on one elbow, the blanket falling back to reveal fading tattoos running the length of his naked arm.

'My boat?' he asked quietly.

'Ay, they've spotted it, I expect.'

'Arme Schweine,' the German muttered to himself, watching the old Tommy sailor shuffle painfully to the door in his heavy seaboats. He reached up stiffly and pulled down his duffle-coat, which hung there from a nail.

'Do you think you will be sinking it?' he asked.

The old man struggled into his coat.

'I don't know,' he said. 'Perhaps, I don't know.'

Suddenly the German Obermaat felt a great wave of sympathy for the old Tommy sweep over him. They were both men who had gone to sea since their youth and both of them were old – too old for this business. Superfluous in this young man's world. As Thirsk fumbled with the strap of his helmet, forcing his cramped fingers to grip the tough elastic, the Obermaat said gently:

'Why don't you stay here, Englishman?'

For the first time the other man looked at him directly.

'What did you say?'

'Stay here – I say.' He shrugged eloquently. 'They will not be missing you. Yes. Why not sit down now? We can smoke.' He indicated the tin of Woodbines which Erickson had given them. 'Let the young men fight the battle, eh?'

Thirsk's stiff arthritic fingers stopped their fumbling with the helmet strap. He sat down on his bunk and stared across at the German. As HMS *Rattlesnake* shuddered under the impact of the first explosion, the tears began to trickle slowly down CPO Thirsk's leathery sunken cheeks. His last reserves had gone.

'Damn and blast!' Hartmann cursed as the first charge exploded against the U-122's hull and the light bulb shattered above his head. 'So they did have depth charges after all!'

'They can't have, sir,' Lüttjens said as yet another explosion chipped cork and paint off the bulkhead. 'They don't sound like any depth charges I've ever heard. They're – I'm not sure how to express it – too light!'

Hartmann absorbed the information in silence as the 'rain' struck the boat, spouts of water raised by the explosion falling back into the sea. Lüttjens was right. The noise wasn't the same. But even if these weren't the killer depth charges they were used to, they were still having an effect. The sweat was standing out on the crew's pale tense faces. They knew that they were sitting targets at this shallow depth, unable to move without running the deadly electric motors.

Another explosion rocked the boat. Hartmann bit back the pain in his shoulder and stared longingly across at the radio and the operator crouched over it. When would it crackle into life and inform them that air cover was on its way? Or would it remain silent for good? Perhaps his message had not been received at the great listening station outside Flensburg? Or perhaps it had been received and ignored? Goering's Luftwaffe was not apt to risk its precious planes unless pressure were put upon it, and there was bad blood between Goering and Doenitz. Was he risking his own and his men's lives for nothing?

'Lüttjens,' he snapped suddenly, sitting upright again although the pain was terrible. 'We must stick this a little longer. But we'll prepare to surface all the same. If the planes don't come, we surface and we fight.'

'Yessir,' Lüttjens echoed miserably as yet another of the strange projectiles hit them and a fresh group of controls cracked, sending glass splinter flying everywhere.

'Good. How many fish have we got left?'

'Two.'

'Have them armed and readied.'

'The water's very shallow, sir. God knows how they'll act at this depth,' Lüttjens objected. 'Perhaps they won't even fire. At this depth, the firing mechanism might not actuate–'

'*Heaven, arse and twine, man!*' Hartmann roared. 'Don't talk to me like a sea lawyer! It's a chance we must take.' He groaned with pain and felt his aching shoulder tenderly. 'Now for God's sake, get on with it. If those planes don't come in the next thirty minutes, we are going to fight!'

'What do you think, Erickson?' Andrews asked anxiously as the two of them peered over the side and another bomb from Bunts' 'hot potato cart' exploded, sending a column of icy green water high in the dawn air only a matter of yards away from HMS *Rattlesnake*.

'Don't know, sir,' Erickson answered and gave the captain a rare grin. 'But I do know that if they don't frighten the Jerries, they bloody well frighten me! Look at old Bunts over there – he ain't feeling too brave either, by the looks of him.'

The two men glanced at Bunts crouching fearfully over the Holman while Sparks loaded yet another 'depth charge'.

'You know what he's thinking, sir don't you? If that lid goes up too soon, he and Sparks will hand in their badges for harps –

right sharp.'*

'I expect you're right. But the two of them are doing a good job of work all the same. I doubt if the things can hurt the Jerry, but they certainly can rattle them.'

HMS *Rattlesnake* swung about once again and zig-zagged forward, while the crew stared at the water as if they expected the Loch Ness monster itself to appear. Now the ERA and his mate, a rating as dirty and as morose as himself, were piling the last of the home-made projectiles next to Sparks before disappearing out of range.

Andrews bit his lower lip. If the bastard did not come up soon, they would run out of the bombs and then the great plan would have been in vain. They would have to return to Hull with nothing to show for their ten days at sea, save three men dead and a broken CPO who was now good for nothing but the beach. He stared at the first grim diffusion of light edging up above the stark black cliffs of Bear Island. Somewhere,

*The container which contained the grenades was sealed with a lightly soldered lid. When firing the gunner released steam which shot up the tin and also melted the solder, thus allowing the grenades to tumble out and explode.

far off, he could hear a kind of steady droning noise. It caught his attention for a moment. But he dismissed it as quickly, and ran back to the bridge.

'Helmsman,' he snapped, 'take her closer in and a good steady run this time. It's our last chance.'

The three-striper sang out in an imperturbable bass:

'Ay, ay, sir, steady run it is!' As he swung the wheel round, Bunts and Sparks tensed over the Holman for the last attack.

Hartmann broke. The projectiles, whatever they were, were virtually harmless. But he knew the crew could not stand much more of them. Their faces were slick with sweat, their eyes desperate. Somewhere in the depth of the ship out of his sight, a man was sobbing in quiet hysteria. Their breathing was becoming more difficult too and he could see how Lüttjens' chest expanded and deflated as if he were running a long distance race. Beyond him a petty officer had his hand on the flood valve to let in the compressed air for surfacing, holding it with taut fingers as if it were his only hope of salvation.

'Up periscope,' he commanded.

There was an audible gasp throughout the

tense boat. Hartmann staggered painfully over to the periscope as it rose with a hiss and straddled his arms over the rests. The glass cleared. The Tommy was very near now. There she was broadside on to the U-122. They might still have a chance.

'Down periscope,' he ordered as a sudden movement on the Tommy's deck told him that they had spotted the tell-tale white wake of the scope.

'Stand by three and four,' he yelled.

'Three and four ready, sir!'

'Up periscope!'

The glass broke surface again. The Tommy was turning rapidly now; he could see the sudden white fury at her bow. But still she was an ideal target.

'Fire three!' he screamed, feeling the pain threaten to swamp him in agonizing red waves.

'Fire four!'

The U-122 lurched as the two-ton fish smashed into the water, and then again as number four torpedo followed it. Despite the agony of his shoulder, Hartmann kept his eye glued to the periscope. Behind him, Lüttjens was counting off the seconds, hand clenched round his stop-watch. The only movement in the boat was the grey opaque pearls of sweat trickling slowly down the men's pale faces. The Tommy had completed its turn. It was racing towards them, the bone between its teeth.

'What's the matter, captain?' Lüttjens yelled in alarm. 'We've already done ten–'

His words were drowned in a thunderous explosion beneath the U-122. A blinding blue flame seared through the boat. Controls shattered. Glass splinters shot through the air. The lighting flickered, went out and came on as a gyro compass slammed against a bulkhead like a shell.

'Surface!' screamed Hartmann.

The ratings jumped to the wheels. Spinning them round frantically, they drove the water out of the boat. The air thundered into the tanks.

'Get ready to man the gun… Essels, stand by with those diesels!'

'Let me take over, captain,' Lüttjens cried and tried to prevent the captain from staggering towards the ladder leading to the conning-tower.

Hartmann, the blood pouring down his side, pushed him away savagely.

'Leave me alone,' he snarled, swaying dangerously. 'Don't touch me, Lüttjens!'

The conning-tower broke the surface and

the first explosion threw him across the lip of the hatch just as he had heaved himself on to the dripping bridge. He screamed as the red hot piece of shrapnel struck him squarely in the face.

'Captain!' a faraway voice yelled.

Blinded, he thrust out an arm.

'Get out of my way!... Do you hear me – get out of my way!' He clambered to his feet. The world had become a red darkness. He tried to raise his right arm to wipe his eyes clear. But he had no right arm. He staggered against the side of the conning-tower. 'Where are you, Lüttjens?' he cried. 'For God's sake man, point me in their direction – *Lüttjens!*'

But Leutnant Lüttjens, the broad-faced East Frisian, whose one ambition for this cruise had been a safe return to his blonde fat Wiebke, was already crumpled dead on the deck below. Thus Leutnant zur See Heiko Hartmann faced up to the victorious enemy, blind, dying, and in the end, alone.

A great roar went up from the men on the deck of HMS *Rattlesnake,* as the U-boat's own torpedo blew her to the surface. It had obviously refused to function after leaving its tube, but had been actuated by the water pressure as soon as it had sunk deep enough. Now the grey wolf was there at last, obscene bubbles of air bursting all around her, gouts of oil spread outwards into the water from her buckled plates.

'Stop ports,' Andrews ordered, 'wheel amidships.' The U-boat was obviously finished, but this time he was going to take no chances. 'Open fire!' he yelled.

A hail of fire swept the length of the stricken boat. Thick, black oily smoke poured from her.

'Steady as you go – half ahead together!' Andrews bellowed above the frantic chatter of the Oerlikon, as they came in for the kill.

The U-boat's mast had toppled over at a crazy angle sawn off by the 20mm shells. The bridge was a broken shambles and fire had begun to crackle along her stern. Blinded and totally out of control the U-boat smacked into the rocks of the bleak black shore of Bear Island. It shuddered violently and heeled over to one side. Men were pouring from the conning-tower, pushing aside the white-capped figure who might have been the captain.

'Port fifteen, steer one-eight-oh – slow together,' Andrews rapped. Despite the danger of the rocks he was not going to let them escape. 'Get those men!'

The Browning gunner needed no urging. He switched his twin weapons round on the men trying to abandon the U-boat. One rating dropped to the wet rocks and started running frantically through the knee-deep water. A burst caught him in the small of the back. He flung up his arms and flopped into the water. The Oerlikon gunner swung his fire from the conning-tower, now a mass of flames, on to the bows where the terrified survivors were clustered, as the hated grey hull started to slide under the dark water in a frenzied upheaval of oil and air.

'Cease firing – cease firing!' Andrews screamed above the din, vaguely aware of a new sound impinging on his consciousness. The grey wolf was beaten; the wonderful moment was over. Now his elation was replaced by curiosity, as the flames, licking up around the shattered conning-tower, revealed the tall figure in a white cap and sodden uniform jacket, standing up there alone, the last man alive on the U-122.

As the strange noise grew louder, Andrew Andrews stared at his unknown enemy and wondered what must be going through the German's mind now that it was all over.

'Sir!' a warning voice came from somewhere on the stern, but failed to penetrate his consciousness. His eyes were still fixed on the German. Should he attempt to rescue him? he asked himself. No, the German would want to go down with his ship and it was better that the Jerry remained faceless. In war it should always be so. Brought into contact with him, the German would be stripped of his menace. He would become a human being to be offered tea and cigarettes and would make the victor feel somehow cheated of his triumph.

'Sir,' Erickson screamed frantically, 'Jerry planes!'... 'Here they come!'

And the last sound the blinded young German captain heard, as the flames rose up to consume him, was the roar of engines as three Junkers 88s swooped down over the sea.

Deafened by the roar of the German planes zooming in at sea-level, the engine room frantically attempting to build up power as they backed away from the sinking U-boat, the crew of the *Rattlesnake* were caught completely off guard by the torpedo. It slammed viciously into her bow, and blew them away. A blast of heat surged up from below and swamped the bridge as the water tore into the engine room. From the voice pipe came the terrified scream of the Scottish ERA as the burning hot steam engulfed him.

'Sparks,' Andrews bellowed at the radio-man running below on the crazily tilting deck, its plates already beginning to buckle in the tremendous heat from below. 'Signal on R/T – plain language … give our position Bear Island. Quick, man!'

Sparks needed no urging. He doubled away swiftly, finding however that his speed was reduced by the violently tilting deck.

Erickson struggled across to Andrews, bleeding from a cut across the eye. He was panting hard, but his face was as steady as ever.

'Abandon ship, sir?' he asked, as if he were requesting permission to urinate in the 'pig's ear' – the urinal at the side of the bridge – instead of making the terrible suggestion that HMS *Rattlesnake* should be sacrificed to the sea.

It was the first time that Andrews had even thought of the possibility, but as the Junkers came roaring in again, their machine guns chattering, he knew that there was no other course left open to him.

'Yes, Petty Officer, get the boats out. Wait

for my signal, then over they go. Get on with it!'

Erickson wiped away the blood with a dirty hand.

'Ay ay, sir, I'll ready them now.'

Suddenly Andrews remembered the ship's papers and the Admiralty codes. As the men on deck scattered wildly under the German fire, he darted into the companionway. Other men were battling their way up on deck, their eyes wild, their faces distorted by their exertions and the experiences of their situation, but not by panic.

Andrews buffeted his way through them, darted into his cabin and seized the papers. He looked round the evil-smelling little hole which had been his home for these last seven days. Anything to be taken? There seemed to be nothing he wanted. He ran out again and nearly bumped into the little Jerry POW. He was leading a blank-eyed, toothless CPO Thirsk by the hand. Andrews stopped.

'What's going on, Chief?' he cried. Despite the emergency he was alarmed at the CPO's appearance.

Thirsk did not reply, but the German answered for him.

'*Keine Angst* – no fear, Cap'n, I shall look after him!'

'Good.' Beneath Andrews' feet the deck tilted and then shuddered alarmingly. 'Come on then – no time to waste.'

Just as they reached the ladder which led up above, they heard a violent rending noise. Andrews swung round. The bulkhead had split open like an overripe peach. The water was pouring in. In an instant it was up to their waists, swirling around them in a wild white torrent, pulling them off their feet. Andrews pushed the German and Thirsk in front of him, feeling the sucking of the water growing stronger.

'Get up there – for Christsake!' he yelled.

Hurriedly they mounted the ladder, the German hoisting a stiff-kneed Thirsk up behind it. As the water swung boldly at Andrews' chest, he sprang upwards out of its grasp and grabbed a rung of the ladder. Next instant he was hauling himself up and out on to the wildly tilting deck, into the cursing, chaotic mass of men preparing to abandon the stricken *Rattlesnake*.

And then fate came sweeping down over the sea. Within seconds visibility was down to fifty yards and the tug was enveloped in its clammy, grey mantle. The sailors frantically scrambling down into the boats, the lead Junker broke off its bombing run abruptly.

Andrews, the thick code-book clasped to his soaked chest, stopped suddenly at the head of the rope-ladder, and looked upwards. The Germans were up there all right. He could hear them still droning round and round frustratedly, looking for a gap in the fog so that they could plunge down for the kill.

'Sir,' it was Erickson in number two boat. 'Sir, you'd better get your skates on! We haven't got much longer!'

As if to lend emphasis to his plea, the *Rattlesnake* shuddered violently. Andrews bit his cracked bottom lip: what should he do? Above him the drone of the German planes was getting fainter and fainter. They had given the *Rattlesnake* up as a bad job. Probably they knew they had dealt her a death blow and were eager to escape the Arctic fog.

'Sir!' Erickson yelled again as the *Rattlesnake* gave a belch and great bubbles of trapped air began to explode on the debris-littered surface. 'For Christssake – come on!' Andrews hesitated no longer. With an angry grunt he tossed the weighted code-books into the water where they sank immediately, and swung his leg over the side, leaving HMS *Rattlesnake* to her lonely fate.

DAY NINE

'That damned Tommy must be stopped before he reaches his home base... Destroy him, Heinze, *destroy him!*'

Admiral Doenitz to Lieutenant Commander Heinze, CO 3rd E-Boat Flotilla

'And now, I'm going to shitting well sing,' the drunken blonde Norwegian whore announced above the roar in the smoke-filled crowded mess party, 'whether you sodding Fritzes like it or not!'

Staggering dangerously, dressed now solely in black sheer-silk panties and somebody's seaboots, she pushed her way through the drunken officers of Number Three E-Boat Flotilla,* pushing away the greedy hands which attempted to slap her black-clad buttocks.

'Get a load of that rigging she has on her, Kapitänleutnant,' young Otto Bastian chuckled. 'She could use that tackle for

*German motor torpedoboat.

better things that singing!'

Kapitänleutnant Heinze, the commander of the Number Three Flotilla, whose idea it had been to bring the whores from the Narvik Officers Brothel to liven up the traditional party, took his head from between his whore's naked breasts and looked at the blonde. She had taken a swig of the pianist's beer and spat it almost immediately into the nearest flower vase. The yellow flowers it contained were already beginning to wilt in protest. Now she was harassing the young sailor pianist, who had been studying at the Viennese Conservatoire before he had been called up to the Kriegsmarine. She was holding up her big breasts towards him and inviting the embarrassed, red-faced sailor to, 'have a suck at them', instead of his 'shitty stale beer'.

Heinze grinned drunkenly and told himself that Navy HQ down in Oslo would shit a brick if they knew how the officers of the 3rd Flotilla were spending the last two days of the old year in their remote Troms base. But then, he reassured himself, those champagne admirals in the Norwegian capital usually didn't know their arse from their elbow. He sighed contently and began muzzling the whore's right nipple again.

The blonde began to sing in poor imitation of Sarah Leander, Berlin's current singing star,

'Tante Hedwig, Tante Hedwig, ich hab' die ganze
Nacht probiert und mein ganzes Oel verschmiert...
Die Nahmaschin' – es geht nicht!'

'*Pfui*,' a drunken, red-faced engineer attached to Bastian's boat cried and whistled through his fingers. 'Take yer drawers off instead!'

'Yeah, take yer drawers off!' the cry was taken up everywhere.

'By the great whore of Buxtehude!' young Bastian yelled, 'can't anyone tie a knot in her neck.'

Before anyone could stop him, he had sprung to his feet, scattering glasses everywhere among the screaming whores and taken a running dive into the mess's greatest pride: the huge aquarium tank which they had looted from the local Norwegian fishery research station. The young officer came up, spluttering frantically, scattering gasping goldfish everywhere on the floor.

'Life-boat drill!' he roared drunkenly. 'Everybody stand by for life-boat drill!'

The whore in the black silk panties continued to sing, while a group of laughing red-faced officers jostled each other to make waves, slipping on the wet floor and goldfish, and Leutnant Bastian gave a drunken parody of the standard drill.

It was at that moment that the mess steward opened the big doors and stood there, blinking furiously, his glasses steaming up in the thick heat. Voices, thick with schnapps and beer, threatened him with a sudden transformation into a singing tenor if he didn't close the door. Someone threw a goldfish at him. He ducked quickly, quite used to the antics of the young officers when they were drunk. Then he spotted Heinze and, hurriedly dodging the importuning hands grabbing at his trousers, made his way to him.

'Sir,' he said urgently, as yet another drunken officer grabbed at his braces.

Kapitänleutnant Heinze raised his head from the whore's nipple.

'Holy strawsack, man, what is it?' he cried angrily. 'Can't you see I'm busy!'

'Of course, sir... But it's the phone!'

'Oh go and jam it up your ass, man!'

Heinze turned to bend his head over the whore's breast again.

'But it's important, sir. It's the BDU from Mürwik.'*

'What!'

'The BDU,' the unhappy steward repeated, fighting off the drunken officer's hands.

'Great crap on the Christmas Tree!' Heinze stood up suddenly. 'Why didn't you say so, man, right away?'

Leaving the whore sprawled out on the wet floor, he pushed his way through the crowd to the door. It did not pay to keep the Big Lion waiting.

'Doenitz!'

Heinze recognized the icy, determined voice at once.

'At your service, Admiral,' he snapped formally, quickly adjusting his tunic.

'Good evening, Heinze. Thank you for coming. What I have to say to you has already been cleared with Admiral Raeder.** So you can take it as an official order. Clear?'

*Abbreviation for *Befehlshaber der Unterseeboote* (Commander of the U-boats).

**The head of the German Navy.

'Clear as thick ink,' Heinze told himself. 'Yessir. Quite clear, sir.'

'Good,' said Doenitz. 'Listen to this then. Over the last forty-eight hours my wolf packs have destroyed the British convoy PQ 8. Unfortunately my Lords have also suffered severe casualties. During the afternoon one of my boats, commanded by a Leutnant. Hartmann, signalled off Bear Island that it was being attacked by a Tommy escort vessel. We sent air support immediately.' Doenitz sighed. 'That help came too late to save young Hartmann. Before those damn fly boys could sink the Tommy, he had escaped in a sudden fog. Are you still with me?'

'Ay ay, sir,' Heinze said, wondering what all this was leading up to.

'Well, according to the weather people, we'll be socked in here for the next twenty-four hours. The Luftwaffe has grounded its planes in Norway. So it looks as if the damned Tommy will escape if you can't stop him.'

'The Third, Admiral?' Heinze had suddenly sobered up.

'Yes. Your E-boats are the only craft close at hand which can tackle the problem.'

'But we're stood down sir and two of my

craft are not in good enough shape to go to sea. The weather up and around North Cape has been–'

'I know all that,' Commander Doenitz interrupted harshly. 'But this is a very special case. You see, both young Hartmann and his brother Colonel Hartmann of the Luftwaffe – also lost on this operation – are the only sons of General Hartmann.'

For a moment the E-boat officer was puzzled; then he remembered.

'You mean, Major General Hartmann of the 105th Infantry Division, sir?'

'I do indeed, Heinze. General Hartmann who will no doubt conquer Moscow itself within the next seven days.' He lowered his rasping voice significantly. 'And I'm revealing no secrets when I say that Hartmann is highly thought of in the Führer's Headquarters. When I was at the Wolf's Lair last week, the place was full of talk about him. Do I need to say more, Heinze?'

Heinze realized what Doenitz was hinting at. It was well known among the regular officers of the Kriegsmarine that the Big Lion was determined to unseat Raeder, the advocate of the big ship approach to naval warfare. According to Doenitz, the war at sea could only be won by one hundred per cent concentration on the manufacture and employment of U-boats. But in order to get rid of Raeder, Doenitz needed the support of the Führer, who until now had shown little interest in naval affairs.

'You can well imagine, Heinze,' Doenitz continued, 'what General Hartmann's reaction will be when he discovers that not only have his two sons sacrificed their lives in this operation, but also that the enemy ship which killed the second one was allowed to escape by the Kriegsmarine. It wouldn't look good for our arm of the service – not good at all.'

'And my role sir?' Heinze asked, knowing that he was committed to the operation, New Year's party or no New Year's party. The Big Lion wanted to protect his reputation for efficiency at the Führer's HQ when the victor of Moscow was received there by the Leader to receive the oak leaves to his Knight's Cross (and the bad news about his sons). Doenitz was not going to leave any avenue open for criticism.

'Your role, Heinze? I'm signalling you full details of the Tommy's present position and likely course. They should be with you inside the hour. Your role?' he repeated the question. 'It is very simple. That damned

Tommy must be stopped before he reaches his home base, preferably off Norway. Destroy him, Heinze, destroy him.'

His heart sinking, Kapitänleutnant Heinze snapped to attention and barked:

'Zu Befehl, Herr Admiral!'

The wild party was wound up in minutes. Heinze flung open the big doors. A wave of smoke and noise hit him in the face. The drunken whore was still singing her lewd song. But now she was minus her panties, which the embarrassed pianist was wearing around his head like a mob cap.

'Gentlemen,' he bellowed, noting automatically that the whore was not a true blonde. *'Darf ich um Ruhe bitten, meine Herren!'*

The music trailed away. Sweating red drunken faces turned curiously in his direction.

'Gentlemen, we have a mission. Would you ask your ladies to leave the room, please?'

'Pfui!' young Bastian yelled, sitting up, dripping wet, in the glass tank, a couple of goldfish gasping their last on his lap. Another couple protested, but most of them knew from the look on the Flotilla Commander's face that the balloon had gone up

and the great New Year orgy was over.

The giggling, half-naked whores began to file out, tottering dangerously on their high-heeled shoes. Greta, clutching a blouse to her big breasts, looked up at him and pouted:

'Do you love me, darling?'

'Sure, I love you. Here's twenty kroner.' He shoved the note in her outstretched hand and pinched her buttocks as she passed.

'And don't forget to keep your legs crossed till I get back,' he called after her. 'I don't want to be working on wet decks then.'

As the big door closed behind her, the smile vanished from her rouged whore's face.

'Fritz bastard!' She muttered to herself and began hurrying into her clothes, oblivious to the wide-eyed looks of the young German sailor-servants.

Ten minutes later she was in the yellow-lit back room of the slovenly little tavern just outside the German naval barracks, telephoning under the watchful cautious gaze of the local resistance men.

'Get me Fru Oeynebraaten quick. It's urgent.'

One hour after she had contacted Fru Oeynebraaten, a lone man was crouching on a remote mountainside overlooking the little coastal town. Despite the deep snow, the night air was heavy with the odour of reindeer moss, but the SOE man had no time for the fragrance. His eyes were on his skis as he tapped out an urgent message to London headquarters.

'Action off Bear Island … Third E-boat Flotilla for sea duty immediate … Locate and destroy British craft … Believed name … C-R-A-C-K-L-E-S-N-A-K-E…'

'*What* did you say, young man?' Admiral Fox-Talbot snorted, shading his eyes against the glare of the lamp on his paper-littered desk.

The aide flushed. Before the war he had been an assistant lecturer in English Literature at University College with a rather nice beard and respectful students. It went down badly to be called 'young man'. But he dared not tell the hot-tempered Flag Officer-in-Charge, Hull that.

'Coastal Command signals that they can't spare a plane, sir,' he repeated his message. 'There's a big flap on off the Dutch coast apparently. They say they need every plane they've got for the rescue op.'

Admiral Fox-Talbot was glowering up at

him and he could hear him breathing hard as he continued uneasily:

'So I'm afraid that – if this *is* HMS *Rattlesnake* – she'll have to make out the best she can under her own steam without the help of Coastal Command.'

'You think so?' Fox-Talbot said ominously. 'You think that they should make out the best they can – in those temperatures – with the Huns throwing everything plus the kitchen sink at them. My God, man, have you ever sailed those seas in winter? It's sheer hell, I can tell you.' He flashed a contemptuous look at the aide.

'But we don't know that the message from Norway is okay, sir. *Cracklesnake!* I mean even the chaps in Room 39 had their reservations–'

Admiral Fox-Talbot waved him silent.

'That's the trouble with you intellectuals,' he said. 'Too many damn reservations. In the Royal, it's always been either pee or get off the pot. You clever chaps want to do both. I'm not going to allow my sailors to die like miserable animals out there with no attempt made to save them. Get me that damned Coastal Command station on the blower.' He drew a deep breath. 'I'll sort the Brylcreem buggers out.'

The Coastal Command duty operator was polite but pessimistic.

'I don't think I could wake up the station commander like that, sir. The Group Commander only went to bed an hour or so ago and he has an early call for zero five hundred hours. It's the big flap, you know, sir.'

'How very interesting,' Fox-Talbot said, and in a voice that was sweet reasonableness itself, he asked: 'I don't suppose you could try to get the duty officer, could you, operator?'

'Of course, sir. I could do that. But it might take a little time, sir. He's just finished checking the sentries. Now he's probably off to the cookhouse for his cocoa. Most of the duty officers like a cuppa around now.'

'Listen operator,' Fox-Talbot exploded while his aide blanched at his side, 'if you don't get that damned duty officer of yours on to this line in one minute flat, I'm coming up to Scotland personally to stick his mug of cocoa up your fat Royal Air Force arse – full of hot cocoa too! Now move!'

The startled operator moved. So did the station duty officer. He woke the station commander. The Group Commander wasn't too happy at being awakened just when he had dropped off to sleep after an exhausting day, but he did his best. He gave the irate Admiral a dozen good reasons why he could not spare a plane to find the *Rattlesnake*. The Admiral demolished them with the same blunt forthrightness he had used on his academic aide. The Group Commander blustered. He would like to help, but his crews were exhausted, and there was a big op on the morrow. Over Holland. Bomber Harris had ordered all Coastal Command planes to stand by to pick up his crews who went down in the drink. Max effort!

Admiral Fox-Talbot told the Group Captain what he could do with Bomber Harris and his Wellingtons. The Group Captain grew angry.

'Sir,' he snorted, 'I'm not used to being talked to like that – even by officers senior to me. Nor do I like to hear Bomber Command being spoken of in such terms. I am afraid I'm going to have to refuse your request and – in addition – report this conversation through channels to my superiors.'

Admiral Fox-Talbot sighed and clapped a

big hand over the mouth-piece.

'Would you mind leaving the room for an instant,' he said to the aide.

What the Flag Officer-in-Charge, Hull said to the Group Captain that night, his aide never found out. All he knew was that when he was called back into the Admiral's office, his chief was still talking to the Group Captain in Scotland, but now his tone was friendly and affable. Fox-Talbot slipped his hand over the mouthpiece:

'Immediate,' he whispered, 'a dozen cases of that gash Scotch whisky – the awful stuff – to a Group Captain Lockney. I'll give you the field Post Number later.'

Beaming in the knowledge that two Sunderlands were already on their way to find and protect the *Rattlesnake* – Admiral Fox-Talbot exchanged a few final pleasantries before asking:

'What did you say, Group Captain? Happy New Year!... Naturally, I'd quite forgotten. The same to you and let's hope that 1942 is better than this bastard has been, eh? Well, thank you again. I'll be sending you details of the other thing in due course. You understand me? Addressed to you personally care of your mess. Goodbye now.'

He clapped down the phone. The smile

disappeared from his tough, handsome face.

'Pompous bastard,' he snorted. 'And a crook to boot. All right, Jones, get on to that firewater for him – and I hope it knocks his liver for six.'

'Yessir.' The aide could never bring himself to say, 'ay, ay, sir.' It sounded so absurd, just like a character in some Errol Flynn sea picture. He had just reached the door when the Admiral called.

'Oh yes – by the way – who is the skipper of the *Rattlesnake?*'

'A Lieutenant Andrew Andrews – Royal Naval Voluntary Reserve, sir.'

The Admiral's brow creased into a frown for a moment.

'Wavy Navy chap, eh?' He shrugged. 'Can't say I remember him – one sees so awfully many of them. No matter. Wherever he is this night in that old tug the *Rattlesnake,* he can count his lucky stars that he's got the Royal on his side. Now we can give the Huns a run for their money at least.'

He waved a hand at the aide.

'All right, Jones, run along now while I get on with this awful stuff.' As the aide went out, he sighed wearily and bent down to face the mass of paperwork needed in the planning of the next Murmansk run, wishing fervently he were a young man again, running a collision course with the German Navy.

The night hours passed leadenly in the two boats, hobbled together by a stout rope. Erickson and Andrews kept them going till after midnight by making them sing and exercise every ten minutes. But in the end when the three-striper in charge of the other boat groaned:

'Can't you put a sock in it, Petty Officer and give us a bit of a break,' he and the Captain relapsed into silence.

Erickson kept himself busy for a while thinking about what kind of meat he would buy with the supplementary ration cards they gave to shipwrecked seamen; then becoming bored with the problem of pork or beef sausages, he switched to girls. That subject kept him busy for a murderously long hour, as he worked his way from the girl next door who had first showed him 'it' as they had played 'doctors and nurses' through the two landgirls he had at the same time in a James Street air raid shelter during a Jerry attack, to the well-endowed wife of an aircraft worker on night shifts at

Brough, with whom he had been sleeping.

It was about then that the little German reported that Thirsk had died. With fingers that felt like enormous, stiff sausages, Andrews sought the old CPO's pulse. He couldn't feel anything. He listened to his chest. Again nothing.

'He's had it,' Bunts said gruffly. 'Better bang him over the side.'

'Shut up, Bunts,' Andrews answered. 'I've not got a mirror to check if he's still breathing. I'm not going – well, I must be satisfied the Chief's dead before we bury him.'

Bunts wiped the end of his dripping nose contemptuously. With Erickson's help Andrews laid the old man out at the other end of the little boat while the German POW sobbed softly, the tears running down his sunken cheeks.

Time passed. Thirsk's outstretched right hand bobbed up and down with the gentle swell, as if he were really still alive. In the faint light, Andrews could just make out the swallow tattooed above the name of his wife 'Meg'. After a while Bunts said:

'Well, at least we could take his duffle off him – he won't need it to keep him warm where he's going Skipper.'

'All right, take the bloody thing!' Andrews snapped with a sudden burst of temper. 'Gods knows what you've got for a heart, Bunts. Bloody stone, I expect.'

Bunts clambered across the others and with some difficulty stripped off the duffle coat. When he sat down again, he offered half of it to Sparks to cover his legs. Sparks refused with a curt shake of his head. Bunts shrugged:

'All right, be proud, mate. But don't come crying sodding stinking fish to me when yer bollocks are freezing off.'

Thereafter, despite the freezing cold, they fell asleep one by one. When they awoke again, just before dawn, CPO Thirsk had gone, disappearing from their midst quietly, and without fuss, just as he had lived. Erickson and Andrews searched the swell around the two boats and asked the three-striper for his aid, but Thirsk had gone for good.

'Poor old bugger,' Erickson commented thickly. 'He deserved something better than that. All right,' he commanded, raising his voice, 'no more kipping for anybody. We're going to stay awake – and alive! One, two, three – Now this is number one, and he's got her on the run, roll me over–'

Wearily they joined in:

'Roll me over in the clover, in the clover, roll me over, lay me down and do it again…'

But when the dawn finally came, it revealed no warm swaying field of clover; just the harsh Arctic seascape, bounded by the black cliffs of Bear Island on which the gulls rested in their thousands, cawing hoarsely as if they were already savouring the flesh they would pick off the dead bodies of the men far below. And then Sparks raised an excited cry which set all their hearts beating faster with new hope.

'Hey, lads, look over yonder… It's the old bitch!' He pointed a trembling finger to their port.

A clumsy black shape was coming slowly but surely out of the shreds of grey mist which still hung about off Bear Island.

'Oh, my holy Christ!' Erickson hissed, 'it's the *Rattlesnake!*'

As they rowed closer to the *Rattlesnake* through a sea littered with debris – cork life-jackets, air-tight tins of duty-free Capstans, a bosun's chair, a couple of empty turps bottles from the engine room – Andrews took in the damage. The rusty old tug was lying pretty low in the water with a great V-shaped gap of some twenty feet at the top near the buckled deck, becoming narrower below the waterline. But she was still buoyant. She had fought the elemental force of the sea and had apparently won – thanks to the skill of the Clydebank shipbuilders.

'Ship oars!' he commanded hoarsely.

Gratefully the crew ceased their exertions. Behind them the three-striper's boat came to a similar halt, while Andrews stared curiously up at his old command. At that moment Andrews felt lonely and afraid. There was no Thirsk now to give him advice. It was obvious that the *Rattlesnake* had taken on a lot of water, but being a tug, she did have a much larger pump than a normal ship – a great three ton 8-inch one, powered by petrol, independently of the engines, which the water must have extinguished. It would be a matter of a few hours to pump her dry. That was no problem.

The problem began with the 'patch': the makeshift contraption made of wood and iron bolts and anything else that would serve their purpose, which would have to be thrown over the great hole in her torn bows. If they could succeed in doing that and firing the engines, what then? Could they risk the long haul down the coast of enemy-held

Norway and then the three hundred mile trip across the sea to Scapa Flow? He bit his lip and stared out to sea: empty as far as the eye could see, desolate and uncompromisingly hostile. What the bloody hell should he do?

Suddenly there was an obscene belch as a gigantic bubble of trapped air escaped from the *Rattlesnake's* shattered bows. A gas oven burst to the surface followed a moment later by the fat cook, still clad in his filthy white apron, a ladle clutched in his rigid dead hand, as if he were just about to dish out another portion of his atrocious Irish stews. He had been a 'hostilities only' man, not at all the type for convoy duty, but who had volunteered for it, Andrews couldn't help suspecting because he had preferred his own sex to women, 'a real old nancy-boy', as Bunts had been fond of sneering. But now in his death, he did more for the morale of the *Rattlesnake*'s survivors than his cooking had ever done during his life-time.

The grotesque absurdity of the cook bobbing up and down in the swell next to his gas oven, released the tension that had been built up by that terrible, long night in the open boats and Thirsk's death.

'Will you just get a look at yon silly

bugger!' Sparks gasped through cracked parched lips. 'You'd think he were just gonna dish up some more of that sodding skilly he used to cook!' He threw back his head and roared with laughter.

The three-striper, a man normally not much given to humour, began to laugh too. One after another they joined in, the tears streaming down their unshaven worn faces, while the fat, dead cook bobbed up and down in the swell. Andrews looked at them. Even the little German POW, who had taken Thirsk's death so badly, was laughing uproariously. They rocked from side to side like crazy men, as if they were back in some Hull vaudeville theatre, listening to a comic, and not alone in the middle of the ocean, facing probable death. Suddenly he knew he'd got them. This was his opportunity.

'Lads,' he yelled, 'lads listen to me, I've got something to say! Listen, will you?'

'Oy, pay attention to the skipper, will you, you silly sods,' Erickson bellowed. 'Yer like a lot of stupid schoolkids. Come on now, get yer fingers out, will you.' Swiftly he wiped the tears of merriment out of his own red eyes.

'Thank you, Erickson.' Andrews got to his feet carefully, while they dragged their eyes away from the dead cook and stopped their hysterical exhausted laughter. 'Lads, what do you say to this?' he said eagerly. 'We board the old *Rattlesnake* and try to patch her up. We've got a damn good pump on board, which doesn't need the engines. If we can get her started up, we'll have the *Rattlesnake* cleared of water in a matter of hours. If we can do that, then we can have a bash at getting the engines started and patching up the hole in the bow.' He looked over at the Scottish engineer, his scalded arms swathed in dirty rags. 'Jock here can give the orders, and somebody can carry them out. Can't you Jock?'

'Ay no doubt I can,' the Scot answered dourly, 'as long as I get a wee bit o' help from you lads.'

'It seems a lot of bloody ifs to me,' Bunts said sourly.

'And our course, sir, if we manage to pull it off?' the three-striper asked.

'The course? Why, there is only one course we can take – the shortest course to Hull!'

Standing there in the gently swaying boat, he could see the colour creep back into their haggard pale faces and the light of new hope animate their tired eyes.

'The shortest course for Hull – that's the

ticket, sir!' Sparks cried.

Erickson gave the shattered hulk of the *Rattlesnake* a fleeting glance and his jaw clenched in determination.

'We're right with you, skipper,' he said purposefully. 'We'll get the old bitch back, if it's the last thing we do. Now, come on all of you. Put yer back into it and let's get aboard. We've got a lot of hard graft in front of us.'

DAY TEN

'We've got the sods started at last! The engines are running!'

Sparks to Lieutenant Andrews

Erickson had not been mistaken. The *Rattlesnake* was an unspeakable shambles. Below deck the water was waist-deep, bitingly cold, and jammed with a crazy mess of smashed and twisted metal, as well as a hundred and one personal things belonging to the crew. The engine room, the stokehold and the crew quarters were completely flooded, and, as Andrews had anticipated, the engines were dead. But the great tank containing the vital petrol for the 8-inch pump had not been fractured and after a hellish half hour, up to their waists in the freezing water, it finally burst into noisy clattering life. The pumping operation could begin.

The temperature outside had begun to drop again rapidly and those men engaged in clearing the deck or on look-out were bombarded by flying spray, which cut their exposed faces and hands mercilessly. Soon the *Rattlesnake* was loaded down by several tons of ice which hung in long jagged icicles from the shattered bridge and the torn rigging.

Above deck it did, at least, have the advantage of stabilizing her against the waves, but below it made the task of the men beginning the job of underwater patching even more intolerable. They found that they could stand only fifteen minutes of the job before they had to be relieved: faces white with frostbite, frozen to the very marrow of their bones, writhing with agony once the circulation started to return to their limbs.

But under Erickson's lead, they persevered, building a wooden patch across the gaping hole; building it plank by plank, while the clattering three-ton pump drove the water back slowly but steadily. Each plank seemed to take an eternity to fix with its 'walking sticks' – lengths of iron rod, threaded at one end and bent at the other – before the 'pudding', a roll of canvas, filled with packing could be inserted to caulk it. But as the hours went by, the patch grew, while the water level fell from the men's chests to their waists and finally to their knees. Meanwhile Andrews, Sparks and the burnt engineer fought their own little battle in the icy engine room, now almost dry of seawater, trying in vain to persuade the engines to start. More than once, Andrews felt like collapsing on the wet deck and giving up. But Sparks and the engineer, who was twice his age, kept doggedly on with the frustrating job, coaxing the first tiny, dry cough from the engines, then an asthmatic groan, and finally a ripe belch.

'She's going to go!' the engineer announced confidently. 'Once she starts farting like that, she'll go.' He looked at Andrews, the sweat standing out on his forehead in thick beads despite the intense cold. 'You can go about your business now Skipper. Ay, leave me and Sparks to it. I'm in charge.'

Even at this moment, the old Scot was jealously concerned that no one else should interfere in the running of his precious engines.

'All right, Jock, I'll go and have a look-see at what's happening on deck.'

The world outside had been transformed since Andrews had gone below seven hours before. It was as if the crazily bulging deck were covered in sugar-icing, a blinding white, sparkling and gleaming in the pale

Arctic sunshine slanting over the edge of Bear Island's black cliffs. Here and there a weary sailor was attempting to chip the ice away, but Bunts who was in charge of the party, was crouched over one of the solid fuel blocks from the life-boat, trying to boil some water, his gloved hands held out to the thin blue flame.

At another time and in another place, Andrews would have found the scene beautiful, but not now, when he knew what misery the men trying to complete the patch were enduring. The sight of Bunts warming himself and not lending a hand made him flush with anger.

'What the devil do you think you're on, Bunts?' he yelled.

Bunts turned as if he had all the time in the world, the very way he held his shoulders indicating what he thought of the young skipper.

'Sir?'

Andrews doubled his fists to control his rage.

'What the hell do you think you're doing, boiling water while the rest of us are working like the clappers down there?'

Bunts, his face white and frozen but still contemptuous, answered:

'Well, we've just stopped sir. And it's parky up here. The lads could work better with a drop of char in them.'

'And what about the lads down below – and stand to attention when you speak to me, Bunts, do you hear!'

Bunts stuck out his lower lip obstinately, but he came to a shambling semblance of attention. 'I was just thinking–'

'Don't give me any of that sea-lawyer's bullshit!' Andrews broke in. He picked up a hammer and scraper from the white gleaming deck. 'Get a hold of this and put your back into it, man. Everybody's got to pull his weight on this ship – and that includes you!'

Bunts stared at Andrews, unconcealed hatred in his eyes.

'We've got some rights you know.' He omitted the 'skipper' deliberately and he did not attempt to take the tools offered him.

'Take these tools and hold your bloody lip, will you!' Andrews rapped, colouring even more heavily at Bunts' insolence. 'I'm going to give you three and if you've not got them in your hands by then and doing a bit of graft like the rest of us, Turner, you're on a charge.'

'And who's gonna put me on it?' the sailor

sneered. 'You ain't got your precious CPO Thirsk wet-nursing you now, you know. You're on your own. Just us and you – mate.'

For a moment Andrews was at a loss for words.

'My God, Turner,' he burst out, with a mixture of rage and amazement. 'Don't you know what you're getting yourself into by that kind of talk? Christ man, you're refusing to obey an order on active service – that's mutiny and the penalty–'

'Sod off with your mutiny, mate?' Bunts cut him short. 'Where's yer witnesses, eh? Them bastards over there,' he indicated the others chipping wearily at the ice, 'can't hear you. So who's gonna testify against me? It's your word against mine, mate.'

'Don't keep saying mate to me!' Andrews roared, beside himself with rage. 'And I'll damn well show you whether you can get away–' Lieutenant Andrews never completed the sentence.

The *Rattlesnake* quivered violently beneath his feet. The quiver ceased almost as soon as it had started. But then there it was again – and again. The men chipping ice looked up, startled. Andrews stared at them, as puzzled as they were. The quiver became a beat, faint and hesitant, but a beat all the same. The beat became a regular pulsation. And then they realized what it was.

'It's the engines, sir!' Sparks' jubilant shout preceded him up the buckled ladder. 'We've got the sods started at last! The engines are running!'

Just as the sun went down behind the cliffs, Erickson finished the patch, covering it from top to bottom with heavy canvas to give the planks an additional seal. Hurriedly his team began to support it with whatever they could find in the way of beams and stanchions to prop it up against the pressure of the seawater once they got underway. Andrews, his brush with Bunts forgotten in the moment of triumph, stared at them proudly. It had been his plan and it had paid off. They were going to make a go of it.

'Well, Erickson, it looks as if we've done it, eh?' he commented as the last beam was heaved into place. Erickson sighed with tiredness.

'I hope so, sir... I certainly hope so. And with a big bit of luck we might just make it.'

'Of course, we'll make it,' Andrews declared confidently. He clapped his hand against the wet buckled metal plating. 'If the

Rattlesnake can survive what she went through the other day, nothing can stop her.'

'Ay, well I hope you're right, skipper,' Erickson said slowly, staring at the patch. 'But you know what they say in Yorkshire? The devil shits on the biggest heap – if you'll forgive the expression – and we're a pretty small one.'

'All I can say,' Andrews exclaimed happily, 'is that we'll have to change the devil's nasty habits, won't we? Come on Erickson, let's get the proverbial digit out of the orifice and get HMS *Rattlesnake* underway.'

Sparks' signal to their Lordships was faint but definite. Although the Admiralty failed to pick it up, the listening towers at Hamburg and Flensburg did not. Almost immediately it was transmitted to the bespectacled, chain-smoking expert of the *B-Dienst**.

He went to work on the signal at once. In fifteen minutes he had solved the elementary three-letter code, which was all that had been available to Andrews after throwing his codebooks overboard at the

*The German Navy's code-breaking service.

time of the Junkers' attack. Five minutes later he had typed it out and given the clear-text to the clerk, before settling down to a pleasant evening with the crossword in the *Westdeutsche Rundschau,* a glass of cognac and his favourite Beethoven Symphony on the radio:

'Another day, another dollar,' he sighed contentedly to himself, using the dated phrase he had first heard at Harvard in the twenties.

Thirty minutes later, the Big Lion was running his eye over the brief message, giving the *Rattlesnake*'s position and the amount of damage she had suffered. He turned to his aide:

'Get me Heinze on the phone, will you,' he barked. 'Most immediate and priority number one.'

Heinze called Bastian at once before he set out on another night's fruitless patrolling.

'We've got to pick him up, Otto,' he said eagerly, unable to stop his hands from trembling.

'Who? Winston Churchill?' Bastian asked in the fishdock office, which they had taken over from the Norwegians.

'Do be serious, Otto.' Heinze pleaded. 'You know that if we don't find that shitty

Tommy, heads will roll.'

'I know,' the easy-going E-boat commander answered easily, 'Yours.'

The Flotilla Commander ignored the remark, although it was highly likely that it would be his turnip that would roll; especially now as the SD had discovered the big-breasted Narvik whore was working for the enemy.

'Listen Otto, as you love me, you've got somehow or other to sink that Tommy, or the Big Lion will shit a fine turd and there'll be hell to pay. Do you read me, Otto.'

'I read you, Commander. Don't worry. We're not Doenitz's crappy U-boat heroes. Those shitty sanitation engineers couldn't even find their way into a whore's bedroom. We're the real sailors – we'll find your Tommy for you. End of message.'

'End of message, Otto – and good hunting.'

Five minutes later the E-boat's tremendous motors burst into life, shaking the light wooden craft, as if it would fall apart. From now onwards till they arrived back in port, not even the hungriest veteran would be able to keep a bit of food down at the body-jolting speeds the boat would travel at.

Leutnant Bastian, on the bridge, threw his

white silk muffler across his throat, splashed cheap Cologne across his face to ward off the over-powering stench of the motors, and gave the little craft one final check. The deckhands were at their stations and the gunner was already squatting in the heated seat of his *Vierling* flak.

'Take down the ensign,' he bellowed above the roar of the motors.

Carlssen, another Emden man like himself who had joined the E-boat service because he couldn't stand the boasting of Doenitz's 'Lords', grinned and whipped down the black and white Navy flag. In its place he ran up a pair of red flannel drawers which had once warmed some Norwegian granny's spindly flanks. It was Otto Bastian's personal standard.

But now the 3rd Flotilla's joker's grin vanished. He concentrated on serious business of getting his ship to sea.

'Shut all watertight doors,' he bellowed. 'Let go your stern rope.'

There was a faint splash and the clatter of nailed seaboots as the deckhands hurried to whip the wire-rope aboard before it could fall and foul the propellers.

'Let go your forrard.'

'Full power!'

The lean motorboat slid into the fiord. On the bridge Bastian felt the boat kick as it hit the first wave. His stomach muscles tightened as he watched the last shaft of watery sunlight lance the grey Arctic skyline and vanish. Suddenly it was dark. But on the bridge of the E-102 the green luminous dials illuminated Otto Bastian's sharply handsome face: the hunter, intent on his prey.

DAY ELEVEN

'Abandon HMS *Rattlesnake*... We sailed from Hull you know and that's where the *Rattlesnake* is going to take us back...'

Lieutenant Andrews to an unknown Flight Lieutenant, Coastal Command.

Dawn broke on the first day of the new year cold and vicious. A howling wind was tearing gouts of water off the waves and hurling the spray at the men on the hastily patched-up bridge. It was hardly possible to breathe and the men on watch had to turn to speak. Even the three-striper, manning their only serviceable weapon, the twin Brownings asked Andrews if he could stand down and the young officer granted the purple-faced, shaking veteran permission to do his watch inside the poor shelter of the bridge.

But despite the wind and the huge waves into which the battered old tug plunged with a tremendous concussion that jarred every plate, the *Rattlesnake* kept sailing on, a tribute to the men who had made her two decades before. Once Erickson shook his head in awe as a great gust of wind caught the bows and flung her round nearly forty degrees before she righted herself, and said: 'Holy Christ, sir, you wonder how the old bitch can take it, don't you!'

Andrews turned his head to speak, tugging at the woollen scarf which hid most of his dirty, unshaven face.

'Keep praying that she'll keep on taking it, Erickson. All right, you take over. I'm going to see how they're getting on below.'

The crew's quarters were a sodden mess. Their steel lockers had broken adrift and spilled their contents everywhere among the stove-ashes which littered the floor. The two mess tables had been smashed in the Junkers' attack and strewn the teapots and crockery which had stood upon them with the rest of the mess. Now the off-duty watch huddled among the wreckage, packed in every piece of clothing they could find, damp blankets wrapped round their shivering shoulders.

'Happy New Year,' Andrews said, his breath fogging the icy air. 'Did you manage to find anything to eat?'

'Not a sodding sausage,' Bunts grumbled, not looking up. 'Cold as bloody charity – everything is.'

'Give over,' Sparks said, opening his eyes and looking as if he wished he hadn't. 'There was a bit of bully – found it in the galley, sir. Everybody got a hunk and a biscuit. It weren't much, but it's something.' He raised his voice. 'How we doing, sir?'

'I'll tell you how we're doing,' Bunts cut in before Andrews could answer. 'Bloody awful, that's how we're doing.' He looked up at the young officer, with the same insolent look in his eyes Andrews had seen the day before. 'Why the hell are we going through with this rigmarole. We're never gonna get this bitch home in a week of Sundays. Besides the shitting Jerries will have picked up Sparks' signal now and be on our tail.' He hawked and spat in front of Andrew's feet.

'And what do *you* suggest we should do, Turner?' Andrews forced himself to ask in cold formality.

Bunts jerked a dirty thumb towards the wrinkled German POW.

'Him, that Jerry can parley with them when they come gunning for us.'

Despite their misery, the rest of the off-duty watch turned to stare at Bunts.

'What do you mean – parley, Bunts?' said Sparks. 'What about?'

'I'll tell you, Sparks.' Andrews said. 'Turner wants us to surrender, don't you man?'

'Yeah, and as soon as bloody possible. I've stuck my neck out once too often. I've had a basinful. And the rest of you silly sods have too, if you only knew it.' He looked up defiantly. 'All his lot has got to offer working-class lads like us here is a sodding early grave, take it from me.'

Andrews sensed immediately what Bunts wanted him to do. As the rating began to get to his feet slowly, the grey blanket slipping from his shoulders unnoticed, Andrews knew that Bunts wanted him to strike him.

Years later, when Andrews was a lieutenant-commander and deciding to apply for a regular naval commission, he realized that this moment of confrontation with Bunts was the turning point in his career. Then he knew that if he had lost his temper and struck the other man – whether it came out or not – he would have been finished as an officer and a man. But, fists clenched fiercely, he fought back his burning anger.

'All right, Sparks,' he said, 'I'm promoting you to acting unpaid petty officer. Turner, you're under close arrest. Petty Officer take charge of the prisoner will you. I shall deal with him in due course tomorrow morning.'

It was then that Bunts lashed out with a furious, 'fuck you!' Andrews side-stepped neatly and in that very same instant, Sparks punched his former mate on the chin. Bunts crumpled to the wet deck.

'All right,' the young officer said coolly, 'give him a drink of water somebody and bring him round. You Sparks, take charge of him after that!'

'Ay, ay, sir,' the new PO said with alacrity. 'You can rely on me.'

'Stand by engine room,' Bastian ordered and heedless of the icy spray, focused his glasses over the rim of the bridge. It must be the Tommy, he told himself. Off the port bow, converging on an almost parallel course, the old rusty British tub, with its battered superstructure was rolling from one crazy angle to the other, as if the helmsman were drunk. He ran his glasses along her length, aware that the look-outs behind him were going through the same motions. There was an enormous, roughly patched up hole in the Tommy's rusty bows. Caused by one of the dead submariner's kippers perhaps? Well, that particular sanitation engineer hadn't been too successful in his attempt to sink the battered old ship. Now it was up to the E-boat service to do the job properly.

He lowered his binoculars, and throwing a last dash of the cheap cologne over his white muffler to take away the disgusting stench of oil and metal, began rapping out orders to the torpedo mate. At the same time he swung the lean boat round in a wide arc so that it faced the still unsuspecting enemy midships on.

Leutnant Otto Bastian, the 3rd Flotilla's comedian, had little time for subtlety. His attack-strategy would be simple and dangerous. He would roar in at 70 kilometres an hour, using the boat itself as a direction finder for the kippers. At a thousand metres, he would fire the kippers – they were the FAT surface-running model – and break to starboard immediately. Even the hard-drinking torpedo mate from syphy Sylt couldn't miss at that range. With a bit of luck, he would be in and out before the Tommy gunners were even aware what had happened to them.

'Engine room,' he rapped, feeling the old exultant, hunter's mood overcome him. 'Give me all you've got … full speed ahead!'

The E-102 lurched forward. The roar of the engines was tremendous. A huge white wave sprang up on both sides. The boat's nose was high in the air now. On the soaked deck, the torpedo mate, his black leather coat soaked and gleaming, steadied himself over the firing lever. They were getting closer now. Still the little Tommy tug, with its tall old-fashioned funnel, steamed on unsuspectingly. Three thousand metres ... two, thousand, five hundred ... two thousand...

Bastian, hanging on grimly to the bridge rail, felt his excitement mounting, even though he had done this often enough in these last two years. One thousand, five hundred. Below the torpedo mate from Sylt flung him a hasty look. Bastian raised one finger. A minute to go. The E-102 was hitting the waves at 70 kph. It was as if she were striking a series of brick walls. Still no reaction from the enemy. One thousand, two hundred and fifty ... one thousand.

'Fire!' Bastian screamed above the tremendous roar of the engines. *'One ... Two!'*

The E-boat shuddered. Once, twice. The kippers slid from their tubes, their sleekness gleaming momentarily before they hit the sea. Bastian grabbed his binoculars and focused them on the tug's midships, feeling his hands trembling with excitement. Twin arrows of white were shooting directly at them. There was no hope for the Tommies now. In a moment their tiny steel world would erupt in a flash of yellow and red and come to a violent end. He heard the hollow sound of metal striking metal. An instant later there was the same sound again. Bastian threw back his head and laughed. They had done it. But the laughter froze on his lips. Nothing had happened. Below, the torpedo mate looked up at him in open-mouthed bewilderment. Nothing had happened; the kippers had not exploded!

In his amazement, Leutnant Bastian forgot to break starboard. But the sudden irate stream of white tracer bullets winging his way told him he had to act. As he swung the boat round in a tremendous white boiling curve of water, he realized bitterly why his kippers had not exploded. The 3rd Flotilla's drunken orgy had provided a welcome opportunity for the shitty Norwegian resistance to go about its nefarious business. The FATs had been sabotaged; their warheads had not fired.

'Starboard thirty!' Erickson screamed as the torpedoes hit them. 'Full ahead ... Engine room, can you give us smoke? Yes, I said smoke. We're being attacked!'

Andrews rushed on to the bridge.

'Torpedoes?' he yelled.

'Yes,' Erickson bellowed above the roar, as thick black smoke started to issue from the tall smokestack and the helmsman swung the *Rattlesnake* around as if she were a destroyer and not a battered old tug. 'Over there.'

Bracing himself grimly against the wildly swaying deck, Andrews focused his glasses swiftly. E-102 slid knife-like into the circle of his lenses. A great white bow wave flew up from her stern. Her starboard guard rails were nearly underwater as she heeled in a crazy turn.

'She's coming in for the attack again,' he shouted. 'Stand by for torpedoes!'

Above him on his freezing perch, the three-striper, the spray dripping from his violent red face, lent emphasis to his words with a frantic burst from the twin Brownings. Tracer zipped viciously low over the water.

But Andrews was mistaken in his estimate that the E-boat would use torpedoes. Bastian was taking no more chances, he had pushed the blond-haired gunner from the Vierling flak aside and had taken over the four twenty-millimetre cannon himself. As the E-102 surged forward, the white bone in her teeth, he pressed the elevator pedal. The four thin, air-cooled barrels sank immediately. In the ringed sight, the frantically manoeuvring *Rattlesnake* grew larger. He could see the men on the bridge quite clearly. He pressed the firing button.

The four cannon pounded crazily. Red and green shells cut through the grey air. They riveted a line along the tugs' superstructure. The three striper dropped from his perch like a bird hit on the wing. He was dead before he struck the wet deck. Erickson pushed by Andrews.

'Take over skipper!' he gasped. 'I'm on the Brownings.'

'Erickson–' Andrews yelled desperately.

Too late. The big ex-fisherboat skipper had swung himself up into the swaying perch. Next instant the twin guns started to speak again. Andrews caught a glimpse of slugs striking the water to the enemy craft's portside. And then another burst of rapid 20mm fire ran the whole length of the *Rattlesnake*. He ducked instinctively. The one remaining glass screen in the bridge-house shattered. Beside him the helmsman screamed shrilly and sank to the deck clutching his arm. Erickson fell heavily from his perch and sprawled out in a pool of his own blood. Andrews grabbed the wheel as the *Rattlesnake* swung out of control, and heeled as yet another volley of the murderous fire struck her. Something burned on his forehead. He brushed it away and the back of his hand was suddenly wet. But he had no time for his wound. The E-boat had turned in a wide insolent sweep some five hundred yards away, as if the Jerries had all the time in the world, confident now of their victory. He could see the gunner fumbling with the ammunition pans, as the boat slowed down in the knowledge that the *Rattlesnake* could no longer hit her. Then the E-boat's engines roared into full power again. With the thin yellow Arctic sun behind her, she surged forward towards her prey. She was coming in for the final kill.

Down in the bloody shambles of what was left of the off-duty watch, caught by the fire burst before they could scramble on deck, Sparks was dying next to the dead German. The wizened POW had died instantly. But Sparks fought death violently, as if it were a tangible thing: a mate 'coming it' on some long-drawn out fishing trip in Icelandic waters before the war; a 'matelot' trying to take his 'Judy' away in some Hull dockside pub; a marine looking for a 'bash' in Pompey. Invective streamed from his dribbling lips, as he lashed about him with his shattered arm, throwing great clots of blood everywhere.

'Whores ... pigs ... rotten sodding bastards ... bleeding arseholes...' he cried, enraged at the darkness threatening to overcome him at any moment.

Bunts, lying on the deck opposite him, his legs twisted below his bleeding body at an unnatural angle, clapped his hands over his ears, trying to drown out Sparks' cries.

'Jesus wept!' he screamed, tears of self-pity streaming down his pain-racked face, 'can't you stop that sodding racket, Sparks! Don't you see what it's doing to me?... For Christ sake, Sparks – die!'

It was just at that moment, that the Sunderlands from Coastal Command found them. As they broke through the cloud cover at fifteen hundred feet, the pilots nursing the big four-engined flying boats along at just under 150 mph, the lead pilot, a big ginger-moustached Australian cried into the intercom.

'Well, as I live and breathe! Get a load of that, fellers!'

The crew squirmed round in their cramped positions and stared down at the two little boats, dwarfed into insignificance by the green swaying sea.

'It's them,' the fat navigator who rejoiced in the nickname of 'BB' – all belly and behind – yelled. 'I can tell her silhouette from the charts.'

'Wow!' the pilot breathed in awe, 'you mean the crazy Pommies made it in that. Well, come on fellers, let's get them out of the shit they're in before she sinks of sheer old age.'

The two great planes came in almost silently. Throttles cut back, the muted roar of their engines drifting downwind, they glided down on the E-boat from the pale yellow ball of the sun. Their timing and judgement were superb.

Crazily Bastian swung his guns round and up to meet them. The first Sunderland's bombs came winging down in deadly profusion. They missed, straddled the E-boat on both sides, sending her reeling madly to port so that her mast actually touched the green water, but the follow-up plane did not miss. Its first bomb hit the enemy ship amidships. A gout of white flames shot into the air and licked the length of the craft.

'Oh, my holy Christ,' BB yelled, half in triumph, half in fear. 'They've hit the gas tanks!'

What followed, the crew of the lead Sunderland would never forget. Sailors on fire. Insane human torches, thrashing their uniforms, trying in vain to beat out the flames that engulfed them: flames that ripped at them, tore at them, turning their flesh in a black bubbling pulp. Some flung themselves overboard in their agony. But the water was on fire too and they thrashed around frantically for only a few moments before the roaring flames consumed them. Others lay on the burning deck, with the tracer ammunition exploding all around them in a lunatic fireworks display, their shrinking charred flesh arching their backs into taut bows, skeleton arms flung in a convulsive crucifixion.

Bastian, the flames leaping up the back of his uniform jacket, threw himself over the side in one of the shallow dives for which he had once been famous at his Gymnasium back in Emden. He cleaved the water, the pain of the salt in his crippled claws excruciating. Twenty ... thirty ... forty metres. His lungs could stand no more. He thrust for the surface. But there was no escape from the greedy flames. A last eerie, despairing cry was wrung from the 3rd Flotilla's comedian as they caught and consumed him.

On the shattered bridge, supporting a badly bleeding and deathly white Erickson, hand clasped to his wounded arm, Andrews caught a final glimpse of that terrible face – a black crusted mask, with two bloody pools where the eyes should have been – then it was gone in the shattering explosion, which destroyed what was left of the E-102.

Five minutes later the Australian Sunderland made a perfect landing on the lee side of the *Rattlesnake* to take off Bunts and another seaman, whose leg had been severed, while the plane which had hit the E-102 circled them protectively. Then, with engines roaring, white waves rippling along its bows, the big seaplane taxied up to the tug.

With the helmsman's assistance, Andrews lowered the two wounded men to the boat from the Sunderland. As the radioman bedded the two pathetic wrecks down in the heap of blankets, BB looked at the young British captain above him at the bent rail and told himself that the Pommies must be cradle-snatching to make the thin-faced, haggard boy, skipper.

'What about opening the sea-cocks, skipper,' he called upwards, 'and sinking her? We could take the lot of you off, you know.' He hesitated momentarily while the sailor the Pommies called Bunts moaned at his feet. 'If you'll forgive the comment, skipper, your ship doesn't look to me, as if she could stand much more – and it's a helluva long haul to Scapa!'

The Pommy skipper's reply told the fat navigator that he was not facing a boy, but a man: a man who had wandered briefly into a strange terrible hell and survived; and a man, too, who knew he would have to go into that hell again before this long miserable war was over.

'Abandon HMS *Rattlesnake,* Flight Lieutenant!' the Pommy breathed. 'Good grief, she's going to get us farther than Scapa.' He looked down at the Australian's well-fed concerned face bobbing up and down as his boat moved with the slight swell.

'We sailed from Hull, you know, and that's where the *Rattlesnake* is going to take us back.'

EPILOGUE

'It's 'Ull all right, sir,' the helmsman said confidently, peering through the grey dawn gloom and wrinkling his nose up.

'How do you know?' Andrews asked.

'Because he can smell it, skipper,' Erickson butted in. 'Before the war in the trawlers, the old hands used to say you could smell Hull fifty miles off. The fish, you know.'

'Ay, and other things,' the helmsman said darkly.

Andrews turned to the PO, his arm encased in the dirty sling which the MO had put on it at Scapa just before they had left two days before.

'Well, if we're really there, let's have harbour stations, Petty Officer.'

'Harbour stations?' Erickson echoed incredulously. 'For us?'

'We are a warship, you know,' Andrews replied seriously.

Erickson hid his smile. Harbour stations for the old *Rattlesnake* with her smokestack hanging at a crazy angle and her superstructure patched up at Scapa with odd bits of canvas and rusty corrugated iron that looked as if they had dragged off the great port's scrap heap; not to speak of a twelve degree list to port.

'Ay, ay, sir,' he said smartly. 'Harbour stations it is!'

They swung round the Bull lightship. For an instant Andrews thought of all that had happened since they had last seen it and the men who would never be coming back now: Thirsk, Sparks, big Hawkins, the cock-eyed Hull man, the old three-striper – and the little wrinkled Jerry POW, the unknown U-boat captain, the boy with the white muffler and that terrible charred face, united at last in death.

'Looks as if we're gonna have a reception committee,' the helmsman said as they came closer to the lock gate which would admit them to the inner berths.

Andrews turned to look at the concrete dock lined with civilians in overalls staring at the battered HMS *Rattlesnake* as she limped in at quarter power, her bows so far down that those watching her feared she might plunge back into the greedy sea from which she had emerged like a wraith on this wintery dawn.

'Yes, it certainly looks like it, doesn't it?' He chuckled. 'A bit different from when we left, eh?'

'Hull dockies,' Erickson sneered contemptuously. 'All them buggers is out for is number one.'

But the big, square-jawed PO was mistaken. As the tug came closer, an old man, at last able to read her fading name, pulled off his cap to reveal snow-white hair.

'Three cheers for the old *Rattlesnake*, lads!'

'*Hurrah!*' the cheer rippled along their overalled, oily line, faint and hesitant at first, but growing in volume, to be taken up by the small craft steaming up the estuary in the opposite channel. Sirens joined in shrilly. Foghorns added their basso profundo. Outside the harbour-master's office a youngster in Trinity House uniform, complete with high stiff collar, swung a gas rattle frantically, jumping up and down to celebrate the fact that the rusty old tug had escaped the hungry seas.

'Bloody hell,' Petty Officer Erickson cursed. 'Who would have believed it – they're giving us a heroes' welcome!'

But just as they swung around to back into

the lock, an aldis lamp on shore began to flick off and on malevolently. The grin of joy on Andrews' face faded. It was directed at them, but it was going too fast for him to read more than *Rattlesnake.* He flashed a look of inquiry at Erickson.

'I'll have a go second time round, skipper,' Erickson answered. 'Here we go... *Why not sticking to correct channel? ... why not flying ensign? ... what's decorating bridge, sacks of potatoes?*' He caught his breath and spelled out the end of the signal... *'Report this office zero ten hundred hours to answer my question, Flag Officer-in-Charge, Hull.'* The PO looked at Andrews. 'Now what do you bloody say to that, sir? Hardly here and they start giving us the old bullshit again! I ask you, sir!'

As the HMS *Rattlesnake* nosed her way painfully into the lock, the rising crescendo of the dockers' cheers on both sides of the quay drumming in the crew's ears, Andrews turned soothingly to the irate PO.

'Well, you know what they say Erickson? From hell, Hull and Halifax, may the good Lord preserve us.'

He clapped his hand on Erickson's good shoulder as the telegraphs rang their last order and the motors stopped. In the sudden silence on board, broken only by the cheering and the rush of the incoming water, they stared at each other in relief. HMS *Rattlesnake* was home at last.

The publishers hope that this book has given you enjoyable reading. Large Print Books are especially designed to be as easy to see and hold as possible. If you wish a complete list of our books please ask at your local library or write directly to:

Dales Large Print Books
Magna House, Long Preston,
Skipton, North Yorkshire.
BD23 4ND